The Nightingale's Stone

a novel by
David Mecklenburg

Blue Forge Press
Port Orchard ✿ Washington

The Nightingale's Stone
Copyright 2014
by David Mecklenburg

First eBook Edition
April 2019

First Print Edition
April 2019

For information about film, reprint or other subsidiary rights, contact:
blueforgegroup@gmail.com

Blue Forge Press
7419 Ebbert Drive Southeast
Port Orchard, Washington 98367
360.550.2071 ph.txt

Dedication

For Nisha
and my parents

The Nightingale's Stone

a novel by
David Mecklenburg

Let the drops fall where they may

The Self is revealed in the Sun. Being exists in the Darkness.

Here is the full assemblage of my house of thought: a dark pillared hall of shelves and desks, old quills, enough for a flock of revenant geese. In their awkward mantis walk the pantographs glint and copy across the floor of stars. The vase stands empty save for the dry and desiccated husks of flowers.

I see her on the page, not these letters and language that you read. I am the There-is of my hand. My handprints may last one tide or a million years. This purple hand, with ink of swallows deep beneath my skin; this vellum, once the shield of an old sheep; this ink-blood, galled and tinctured with violet and crimson; this night with its fire and its darkness.

How did I get here? It began before I remember, for that is the world. I am here and must follow the path to the River. There, I shall close my eyes and be a blind woman. Does the coolness of the water, its wetness, give truth to the ells of width or depth? No, I shall swim when my feet leave the bottom.

The pot that boils avarice is made of gold; it is not the metal for my pen. My pen shall be made of steel, pattern welded and thirsty for ink. Gold bends, yet steel is strong and sharp. It splits, bends, opens itself for the ink; it caresses the paper in swift strokes.

Do not let my words be spidery scratches but big ungainly messes. Let the drops fall where they may.

In the Window Hall

High in the mountains, in the ruined window hall, the corner's space comes alive, materializes into a manshape from gray into black-and-red flesh with white veins. From its mutable torso, it grows limbs of diverse composition: two arms, two legs, and a tail. I am held still by no spell save that of fascination and terror abjectly mixed. Naked of skin, thick and moist, he moves like water, like a man made of water, in careful steps towards me. He has a large swinging penis between his legs and a changeable face that resembles a young woman with high cheekbones, then an old man with a grey beard, then a mixture of infant and horse, as though he cannot really make up his mind as to which shape to take. His floppy ears are not like ours; they are large and oak-leaf shaped. They turn to catch the sounds of the wind, of my breath, of my heart. His hair is long, black, and orange, undulating and moving like a river of snakes. He is a beautiful horror.

I must think quickly: What is he? Where did he come from? He must have sprung from a riven tree or some other terrible violence and grew strong upon the slopes of the mountains. He came down into the wide world to eat women, men, and especially children, yet he always returned to this high vale, his home. Here he would sleep through summers, until one fall night, he awoke and found a hall of windows built around him. So he ate the owners and took possession of the stones and the silence. And now I have awoken him.

I say, "Hello, and good evening to you—sir. I am sorry, but I do not know what to call you."

"Who are you? Where are you?" His eyes have not formed completely; they are like oysters: translucent, fragile, and blind. "I know what you are," he continues. "You are a human woman; I can smell you. Past the prime of your kind—forty turns of the Sun, I would say, have passed since you first came into the world. And were tastier." He sniffs the air. "You are bitter-tasting now, and nervous. I can smell your sweat. The fear in you."

"I cannot hide that, sir." I walk away from him. His marvelous ears cup and twitch, rotate toward me. His hair is prehensile—predatory—and it searches upon the floor where one strand finds my leg.

"Where are you going?" The lock of hair is wet and strong, but it is like a muscle, like a cat's tongue, and it curls around my ankle.

"I am going nowhere, it seems," I say. "What place is this? Is it yours? I do not suspect that architecture and construction are pursuits of yours."

"You should know that I ask the questions here," he says.

"What sort of questions?"

"I have already asked you one: who are you?"

"Are we to take to riddling so soon?" I ask.

"That is not a riddle."

"Oh, it very much is," I answer.

"Is it now?" He comes closer still. More of his hair goes around my waist, and he reaches out with his right arm: at the end is a perfect human hand. He touches my thigh, then reaches up and holds my arm as if he is assaying a side of beef.

"You are skinny, sinewy and tough. It is fortunate for you that I am not particularly hungry right now. You would not make a very good meal."

"I am afraid I would not. Well, I am most sorry for disturbing your sleep, or repose, or whatever it is you were doing."

At this he smells every inch of me. He bends low to my bare toes; he sniffs my knees, my crotch, my stomach. He then lifts me, pauses at my breasts. His breath is not cold and slimy but hot and dry, like an oven exhaling. He smells my hair and face. His eyes coagulate, for only a moment.

"Damn these things. They never work right. I should like to see you before I eat you."

"But you said you were not hungry."

"I am not. We shall have to wait."

"What shall we do then?"

"The riddling sounded like a pleasant distraction. Perhaps it can work up my appetite."

"Or diminish it. What is your name, sir?"

"I am not going to tell you that. I can smell you; you have some eldritch scent about you. You are not quite like the others I have smelled and eaten. Are you some sorceress come to destroy me?"

"Some have called me that before. But no, Anton, I have not come here to destroy you. I was led to believe that someone else was here."

"Anton? That is not my name. Why are you calling me that?"

"You do ask the questions here, and quite a few of them. Well, if you won't tell me your name, then I shall have to call you something. And 'Something' does not seem to fit you very well. I can see from your shapes and your diet that you must be a troll. But troll is a generic term, and you are rather … unique?"

"Yes."

"Then I shall call you Anton."

"I do not … how do you say"

"Understand?"

"Yes, that is it. I do not stand under why you use sounds like 'understand.' I am not standing under anything."

"There is the sky above this broken roof."

"You have me there. So I can say I understand the sky and roofs."

"That is a rather precise statement. I was being metaphorical."

"I do not stand under metaphors."

"Ah, but you just did. Surely their taste is familiar to you if you have eaten us before."

"Yes," he says, and yawns. His teeth are long and sharp. Many are blue, some are yellow. A few are white and, as fits his nature, they seem plucked from all the beasts of the earth. There are many rows of them, but the most disturbing is the impossibly long line of baby teeth that forms the inner row. "Yes. I am somewhat familiar with their taste. Your minds seem to be made of them."

"And names are metaphorical as well."

"A name is a description."

"Then you may call me Exquisitely Tough She-Flesh. Very bitter both in the bouquet and aftertaste. My sinews will remain in your teeth for weeks and I produce comprehensive dyspepsia."

"That is a long name. At least it isn't one of those silly names like Daisy. Why on earth would anyone call a girl a daisy?"

"The person that named the girl thinks she is pretty like the flower."

"Then why not call the girl 'Pretty'?"

"Some do."

"Perhaps I should call you Skinny."

"I have been called that before."

"Why Anton? What does that mean? It doesn't mean flower, does it?"

"You are beautiful like a flower, yes. There are carnivorous flowers I have seen with teeth like yours, and there is a Greek word that sounds like that, but you just seem to be an Anton to me. And when I leave here, I promise you that if I ever meet another Anton, I will always think of you."

"You are not going to leave. I will eat you. We will just have to wait until I am hungry."

"Then it is to be the old game, then?"

"What do you mean?"

"You know how this works. I assume the stakes will be the standard ones. I'll eat you if I win and you will let me leave if you win. Now who shall go?" I say.

"...I don't like those conditions. This is my place and I usually do the eating."

"Are you not free to leave then?"

"Well, I don't know. But I cannot agree to those terms"

"Then you are not free."

"I suppose I'm not. Ha, well, that is certainly new," he says.

"Under my terms, we can both win: you either way."

"How can that be?"

"Well, if you eat me when you win, but I cannot eat you if I win, then the terms will not be reciprocal. I would rather eat you, frankly, for you would keep me full for days and weeks. In your belly, I would merely be an annoyance reminding you to eat a proper breakfast and not some thin rind of toast. But under the other terms, I will grant you your freedom if you win, and if you lose, you still win because when I eat you and leave, you won't be here anymore."

"I would rather not be eaten by you. I think letting you go is better. I must tell you that any cheating means I will eat you. This whole thing smells familiar. An old relative of mine once got fooled by a double-talking Greek."

"Then you are doubly lucky."

"How?"

"You have two eyes, such as they are, and you are still in possession of them. Furthermore, I am neither Greek, nor do I have wine. I am sure you can smell that. I cannot get you drunk and there are no sheep here for me to hide beneath, so I won't be escaping that way. I don't plan on gouging out your eye, so really there is nothing here comparable with that situation."

"I like to eat sheep."

"I do as well, so that is something we can both stand under," I say.

"Yes, but I still do not stand under why you are here. For whom are you looking?"

"I was looking for a man. I was led to believe he lived here."

"There is no man here, and who led you? Was it the man who led you here?"

"In a manner of speaking, and that is the riddle I have been seeking. You have now asked the first question. Since this is your hall, I suppose you should have the right of the first question. I do find it strange that you live in such a place, a hall with no roof and full of windows—yet you cannot see."

"You are not answering the riddle."

"Where should I begin? Does a window have a beginning? Where does a hall of windows begin? Windows do not answer. They only allow. Passive in their control of light and memory, they allow me to look through them. They allow others to look at me—to laugh at me while I am naked or while I cook. A closed window is even worse due to the possibility of what lies beyond its shutters and blinds.

"Over there is a window upon the North Sea, and although there are other windows here looking out over other seas, they all contain the water of that first sea. The waves sleep in gray and indigo. Above the water are clouds: the dreams of the sea. I would be lucky to drink from those dreams if they came ashore. I have been thirsty for a very long time.

"Another window looks out upon a wide river. I can see a girl wading into it and her thighs are wet with its blood. She wonders if it will ever be the same river, for suddenly she is a woman. I know she will ask this question every time she crosses that river. Only the obduracy of the flow is certain. But here, close to us is a window that is shattered like a dragonfly's wing. Do you see the mountain it looks out upon?

"No, tell me," he asks.

"I shall tell you, for that is where the answer to the riddle begins. I see a slope scraped by ice and men. Elsewhere, there is impotent verge: meager patches of grass withered beneath salts and metals from the mines that dot the mountain. Yet higher up, there is still a healthy green for sheep and cows. Below an abandoned mine, there is a small cabin. That is where I lived. I can see myself standing outside the cabin in my high-collared scribner's dress with its tight, three-quarter sleeves whose pattern and make prevent me from dragging the cuffs through ink. My hair is a tangled thicket of black they call a raven's clout and my eyes lie hidden beneath a self-cut fringe. Beneath the dress is my own milk-tea skin and skinny body. Down the mountain there is a town in the valley where I stand a head above the tallest man. Amongst the people of the valley, I am different and therefore suspect.

"In the spring, thirteen years ago, the people of the valley were having a festival and dance. I was arguing with myself whether to go down and stand on the periphery of the bonfire or stay in my lonely cabin."

May Eve

Mines have always pierced the Visingberg, or so the miners say. When they exhausted one, they would move somewhere else. The mountain's lodes were rich in many ores, and in time the town of Visingotha grew from a village, and as the knowledge of the engineers and miners grew, so did the complexity of their business.

I am a professional writer, for illiteracy is an epidemic in this world and the fountain of my employment. Like a physician, I treat the afflicted by writing for them. There was an assay clerk there, but the owners of the mining company thought someone of literate capacity with neither obligations nor entanglements should balance him out. I had left those burdens behind in the Free and Hanseatic City of Hagen, the city of my birth.

I had apprenticed in the Great Library of Hagen, but my first lover had disgraced me and so I was forced to leave. In the North, women are more free than they are in the Christian lands to the southwest, but we are not the full equals of men. I could have become a governess or clerk—for

I was well educated—but I could not be bound to an estate or office. I would have entered the servitude of marriage had I wanted that course. And so, in the limited understanding of an eighteen-year-old girl, I chose the path of the purple hand. I was tattooed on my right hand, as are all the scribners of Hagen. The guild gave me a seal and sent me to these mountains. Befitting this rash decision, I owed my situation at the mine to an accident. The previous scribner had been clambering on some rocks, trying to avoid getting his feet wet on a flooded path. One slip brought down a small tumble of rocks, but they were enough to smash his writing hand. His fingers were mangled, cut open, and broken, as though a drunken butcher had tried to cut them off with the back of a cleaver. He had healed, but could no longer write. The mining company offered him a mattock but he refused it. They still mocked his arrogance and stupidity when I arrived and all I could ever discover of him was the bitterness of ashes. He had burned his journals and all his papers in the hearth of the small cabin that I would call home.

The cabin was not mine. I owned nothing there save for my books and clothes. The shallow bed with its straw mattress, always too short for my long legs; the simple table where I wrote; the cooking things; the two tired chairs—even the chamber pot—were owned by the mining company.

Was I above it all? Perhaps in terms of elevation only. Rather, I was outside of it all along with the few cowherds and cheesemakers who were once the only inhabitants of the mountain's slopes.

For eight years I lived this life, alone. There is not much to say of it. I remembered seasons and kept a count of the Moon's cycles, ticked off the days. Behind a loose stone in my hearth was a cache of money that I received from odd jobs and a pittance the mining company gave me. I had been scrimping my money carefully, for I would one day leave Visingotha. Early on, I had been certain of that, but the days, months, and years had diluted my resolve. Once I had accumulated enough for passage off the mountain, I then reasoned that I would need a nest egg to start over. As I wondered how long I would remain in the mountains, my plans and their requisite expenses grew. I had gone nowhere.

No man crossed my threshold for romance—or even just my thighs—and I did not seek them out. I told myself that I had come to the mountain to escape those distractions. I had others.

The few young fir trees spoke in the spring and fall, when shifting winds came and the branches whispered like distant cataracts. Though different from the wind-bent pines near the sea, the firs spoke the same comfort. Some distance from the cabin laid a pond, fed by a spring and brook further up the mountain. An old grizzled, twisted fir tree grew on its banks. How old it was I could not imagine. I often went there to think and look into the pool to see where I may go, and yet all I could see was a reflection of my skinny body, my nose, and the mountain. There seemed to be no secrets, and the only truth was that I would grow old and die alone there. This was the extent of my world: a cabin, the mining office, the mountain and village of Visingotha down below.

That all changed on the eve of May in the eighth year of that world.

I stood outside that evening and watched the stars begin to appear in the east. I could hear the distant sounds of the town: hurdy-gurdies and shawms played dancing music.

Men and women and children were drinking, laughing. A pig was roasting there and I knew they would be eating pastries made from last year's cherries, sugared and preserved. I wanted to see the bright helix ribbons spinning from the women's heads. I even wanted to see beer froth in the men's beards as they spent their wages for a little escape. No one would ask me to dance. Though no one would say it, I knew they all thought I was some ugly witch: a stork of a woman with strange ways and a purple hand.

Yet I also knew that I could join a few people on the liminal edge of the miners' celebration. Helga the pharmacist would be there, along with Benjamin, a cobbler. Perhaps even the sour-faced old attorney would be there: we all shared the ostracism of literacy and supportive roles for the miners and their masters. Some of the Wendish laborers might be there with plum brandy and honey cakes to share. There would be Harzauer cheese to toast on rye bread.

I decided to walk down the old stone path to the town. The shadow of the mountain obscured the mines and twilight lay upon the broken land. As I got closer to the town, I heard a nightingale singing, and the song carried notes like the pink cherry flowers; the melody promised the warmer wind of summer, of some future where things and times were not so cold, but the song was also sad. As any good singer, the bird's song seemed to remind me of my own life, my mother, and therefore long ago. I turned and looked back to my little cabin: my office and my cell. Inside, pressed in the leaves of an old book, was a piece of parchment: an old letter that spoke of my mother's passing. And so my gaze was brought to the West. My grin beneath the sky matured to a melancholy frown. I missed the horizon of the flat North, for that sky was endless, full of possibility. I missed the Evening Star's proud countenance because it lay behind the Visingberg. How long had it been since I'd seen it? From out of the gloom, somewhere ahead of me on the path, I heard a voice:

"At the top of the mountain, I'll wager you can see all the way to Russia and the Urals." It was a deep male voice, soft-textured and immanent. "And the Evening Star shines brightly there, like the Moon, like your face."

He intruded upon the loneliness that had followed me like a shadow: growing and lessening through the course of days and seasons.

"I am satisfied with the Moon here," I said. "But I do miss the Evening Star, for I am not from these mountains."

"I know that, Miss Ludenow, for that is who you are. How could I mistake you? They say, 'She is tall, dark-haired like a raven, and sees great distances. She keeps great magic in her long hands.' Those are daylit hands that scratch out their damned invoices, birth records, and letters, and yet I wonder what her nighttime hands write? Of things and time both distant and terribly near?"

The dream smith laughed then, stepping out from the metaphor of his word forge and holding out his own graceful hand.

"And who are you?" I asked him.

"Pardon me, my name is Modral. Modran Modral."

"You are not from here then, for that is a Breton name."

"I was not born here, but am at home here, and yes, I was raised in Brittany as you guessed. You are a perceptive, smart woman. Beautiful and smart. That is a dangerous combination here."

He was not of the mountain people, yet like the mountains he loomed rather than stood. He was taller than I

was; even in the evening light I could see his eyes were gray like the North Sea in the setting of the Sun. Elegant and carved—not made—his fingers and hands bore witness to the skill of a master sculptor; they were not made from the dull ruddy stumps, broken nails, and puffy fingerpaws the miners shattered against feldspar and granite. His brown hair was shot through with white shards, like light falling from the wings of clouds. His face was handsome and strong.

"Is something wrong?" he asked. "Perhaps it is the breeze carrying the sex of the flowers. They strain so here, for their time is short, like many things upon the earth. I find it hard to breathe their scent, and yet I do, greedily in this rarefied air."

"No, no," I said, and then lied: "Yes, I suppose it is the air."

"I am going that way, across the valley, but my path follows yours, for I guess you are going to the bonfire. May I join you for a time?"

"The path is free," I said.

For a time? The span and measurement of time was impossible as we walked down the path, a pace or so apart, yet abreast. It had been so long, but the thick tenseness of walking with a man felt new again. A man. Not employer, friend, or client but delicious, inexplicable male company.

He is just a man, I tried to reassure myself. I failed.

"You said you were at home here," I said. "I have not seen you before and yet I know most of the people here. I would not forget you."

"I am at home, in a way, for some of my family live near," he answered. "But it is a step in my travels, for I love these mountains at their best: in the summer, of which spring is a welcome prelude."

"Who are you? I am sorry. I beg your pardon. I mean what do you do that brings you here?"

"There is no pardon you need to beg. I am the jack of all trades, Miss Ludenow, and master of none. I have traveled, and now I have returned to homely Visingotha to buy cheese from this valley and sell it in the League cities such as Hagen. Tell me, for unless I am mistaken, that is where you are from."

He spoke this last phrase in my cradle language, and he made the sounds and blutterings of Hagen sound like wonder. It was an easy guess. I had never dropped my hard northern accent, even though I had learned the bouncing, uncouth vernacular of the mountains.

"I am from Hagen. You are shrewd in your guesses, but how do you know my name?"

"Everyone here knows who you are: the weird scribner woman, Ada Ludenow. My business somewhat demanded that I know you, after all. I have some contracts I need notarized."

The path had now joined the main road, stones straight set, beaten smooth and set within a great bed of gravel. He stopped and loomed again. His chin, his ridiculous chin that I wanted to bite as if it were an apple, thrust itself at me in obvious self-assurance.

"I must ask you: Do you miss the Great Library? I can see you there, for your shape is accustomed to the corridors of bookshelves."

"You may think that librarians are the epitome of demure retreating creatures, but they possess the secrets of the world in the lock-chests of their heads. The shepherd is like his sheep, the miner his ore, and the smith his forge; is not a librarian like her books? A book is silent but speaks in many languages, revealing different worlds with each turn of the page so that often one must retrace the steps of leaves to read a previous passage anew," I said.

"Like books, your hands are silent and deft," he answered and then took my hands into his. He studied them, turning them over in the Moonlight. He touched my purple fingertips like dew gracing the optimistic leaves of spring grass. "So you worked there. And then you received the tattoos of the scribners. That must be a tale."

And then he gently let go.

"I did. A long time ago."

My self-remonstration, once new and now old, returned. It was the shame of those words escaping from my mouth, for I had forsworn sharing. I was greedy for my misery: the avarice kept in proud and miserly solitude.

"You must tell me, perhaps tomorrow? I have business with Willi Dörscher—you must know him. I have chocolate from Mexico for refreshment, and I need a notary. I have been searching for a connoisseur of chocolate. Are you both notary and connoisseur? May I come tomorrow, Miss Ludenow?"

"Yes."

I said this to him and looked in his eyes. It was painful, but I did not turn away. I paused a moment longer.

"Please," I said.

"Good night then, Miss Ludenow. Until tomorrow." He smiled and then turned from me.

This first memory of him passed over me but did not leave me. I went to the bonfire and the dance. I remained in the shadows and fought with myself over supposition. Benjamin was not there, but Helga was.

Helga was some ten years older than I and had also emigrated from somewhere else: Mödeburg, which was the closest large city. She was not a beautiful woman, but she had a wide pleasant face and blue eyes. She was short, but of course everyone was shorter than I was. Her hair was the dull blonde of egg-glazed bread and she wore it in braided plaits which gave her a certain gustatory appearance—as though she had escaped from a bakery. In some ways this was true, for like a loaf, her cheek bore a long scoring scar. This was the result of an accident: a splash of her father's chemicals when she had been assisting him in a failure of transmutation. He was an apothecary and alchemist, and thereafter he searched for healing salves for her face and his guilt. They studied books on medicine together and spoke with learned physicians and doctors who said the scar was unchangeable. Yet through this education, she learned her father's trade. She remained unmarried—"unmarriageable," as she put it—and when her father died of a stroke, she left her married sisters and brother who brewed a much more profitable potion, namely beer. Her brother sold the family house but allowed her to keep the alembics, retorts, and other equipment that went with the shop. Like me, she arrived here after being assigned by the mining company.

"You know, Ada," she confided that night, "I was glad when you first arrived in this place, for you could bear the title of witch in my stead. A replaced outsider is never inside, of course, but being secondhand news is not so bad either. But you have been smiling all night now. These people may think differently of you. A very handsome man came into my shop today, asking if we had a notary. I am guessing that he found you."

A Stern Jailer

"So you are one of those people that take the gall of oaks and scratch it onto paper in symbols?" the troll asks me.

"It is called writing. We also use lampblack, pigments, and glue for the ink, which I actually prefer."

"So you are a writer."

"Of a sort, but what I write are other people's words."

"How strange, do you not all share them? You seem to give them away freely, but I gather that when they are scribbled onto a dead sheep or tree they are more valuable."

"Not nearly as much as they should be."

"Your kind's notion of value was something it took me a while to stand under. It left a very heavy taste in my mouth, like gold or lead. What did you do after the bonfire had burned low? Did you find the man?"

"Anton, the phrase is 'understand'."

"What is the difference?"

"People will not understand you."

"That seems preposterous, but I will use your phrase. I wish to understand."

"You will have to let me continue."

"Of course, go on."

"The first night was when the promise seemed most clear, for everything had been renewed. I was afraid to even think that he had changed everything for then the world would come and take it all away. This fear clouded my mind and perhaps it blurs my recollection to this very night. Can I really go back to that first night I met him? Can I hold him in my consideration as I did then? Can I disrobe him in my ingenuity, impress his shape upon my hope, and write the poetry of him in my blood as I did that night?

"I did not eat that night. Not even the food at the bonfire could satisfy my hunger, for it burned and consumed itself. I stood there in the darkness and thought of myself as a small fire burning unnoticed in the daylight.

"How I had squandered those eight years of daylit boredom, nightborn loneliness—never realizing they were the home I had built, timber by timber, mortise and tenon and walled in with the mud-and-wattles of regret. I could not say 'I am beautiful' to myself. As jailer I was stern and comprehensive. I struggled against my solitude being wrested from me by—did I dare say it?—love? A wet, thirsty and a fragile dream, I tried to break it under fears of hubris and shame.

"I still remember the shape of his mouth when he said the word 'beautiful.' I was certain it was the first time someone had said that. I had never been a pretty girl. No one had lied to me when I was younger. And yet, although I do not remember any distinct address, I believe in the somewhere-deeper-than-words that my father once told me that I was beautiful."

"But how can you believe the words if you do not clearly

remember them?" the troll asks.

"The dream of my beauty in my father's voice is a memory that seems pure and without selfishness."

"Perhaps you had always wanted your father to say it."

"Perhaps: for a long time I had been certain that he would tell me when he returned from the far side of the world. He had promised me that he would return 'the day after tomorrow.' I learned that there are thousands of day-after-tomorrows. But the night I met Modran, I had finally found someone who told me I was beautiful and I only thought of the next day."

"Well, what happened the next day?"

Waiting for Chocolate

The next day, after my usual meal of rye porridge, I dusted, swept, and cleaned the little cabin. I tidied the old table, strewn with the tools and slag of my trade: ink wells, blotter, lamp, blank precious linen paper pulped miles away in the flatlands. I restacked the paper and moved it. Then I moved it again. The work was dusty, peevish, and at last I realized I was a mess to be seen.

There was an old frame containing a piece of sheet steel; once, perhaps, it was brightly polished, but time and rust left it as something that simply hung on the wall. I must have noticed it when I was younger, but familiar disuse rendered it as all but invisible. I did not need a looking glass to tell me I needed to bathe; my nose is long and good at smelling. I drew enough water from my well to fill the shallow wooden washtub, and I poured in enough hot water to remove the shock of the cold, but I did not like getting into it. Expecting his knock at any second, I left my dress on the bed and got in the tub. I felt like a naked mackerel trying to fit in a teacup. With a little precious soap, made from sheep's oil and old potash, I felt clean enough.

But he did not knock, and so I dressed and brushed my hair. I was grateful for its fullness and tangles that day, though I would never admit it, because my hair gave me plenty to do. I let it down and put it up several times, and finally decided on keeping it up.

Though it was a holiday, I had letters to copy, and there was a contract and a complicated invoice to the Skrimjager Forge in Thalburg. I smiled when I put my seal to that document. It was fitting because Skrimjager had made my seal in their great furnaces and wrought it upon their anvils. Its workmanship was beyond the deepest imaginings of the smith in Visingotha.

Upon its face fly three swallows in a gyre around my name and they match the swallows on my hand, for a notary is known by the match of design upon her seal and her hand. The birds still thirst for the red wax that melts, transforms and takes the imprint of my name. They also bathe in dark purple ink and leave my name upon the letters and lives that pass beneath my hands. At times they seem to speak to me.

That day was no different.

"The milk is fresh and the cream is yellow and cool in the clay jug, for the cowherd boy brought it this morning. Drink, for you are thirsty and eat of this bread: the loaf caraway, flax, and poppy seeds, and fat rye berries. There are preserves. The butter is folded like lips. Eat. You are hungry."

I obeyed and ate hungrily but drank only a thin tea; the milk I needed for chocolate. I bit my lips and hoped the thick red cherry jam would stain them a deeper shade of desperate.

The morning passed. The Sun moved across the sky, although I knew the earth turned below Her gaze and yet both truths had room within my heart.

Finally, there was a knock at my door. I jumped at it and clambered over my own legs in the tight space between the desk and the door. When I opened it he was gone, but then I realized he had never been there. It was a small commission: an illiterate mother wished for a letter in which I would write her love. She told me that her stumpy son was off fighting as a mercenary in Italy in one of the stupid wars between the King of France and the Catholic's Pope. She was a kindly woman, but my attention wandered. So I composed it myself in the Latin of Horace and Ovid, for I assumed someone there would know the tongue.

I wrote the green on the hills. The goats and cows gave forth honeyweed milk from their teats. The horns of the ram curled in masculine intricacy. The prose caressed the pretty throats of the herding girls: an old pastoral lie. I knew the thick-armed girls actually dug their fingers into the wool of miner's clothes, as they tried to beat and wash away the soot in streams. The girls were tough, broad-ankled, and pregnant by the soldier's friends who had stayed behind, but in the *flumen Latinae* of the letter, they were blonde and bare-calved on the mountains and gazed into butter cups and butter churns for auguries of his return. I let these warmths flow into the words, and hoped there would be an understanding priest of the Catholic faith who might read the words to the unlettered soldier.

The mother paid me with a smile of three teeth. I thanked her, for against the mountains of her life, her love was momentary and therefore beyond the price of men and their silver coins, but she also paid me in such coins, and went barrel-legged down the mountain to post my precious lie. Usually I counted each coin as a step to freedom, even though I had no clear idea of what that meant anymore, but that day I continued to think of the soldier. Would the letter find him? Would his mother welcome him back with the overcooked stodge of cabbage he had dreamt of in the mud of Tuscany? Was he whole or broken?

As the Sun sank, so did my heart. I was no longer immune to the seduction of sugar and sentiment. The mine bell rang a stern bronze tone of release: to remind the wresters to cease their work. After the bell's tones drifted away, I listened to the nightingales. They sang, and as the Sun bade them goodnight, someone answered in trills and whistles.

He had come. He bore chocolate from Mexico.

"You are late," I said, trying to tease the way I had heard other girls do.

"But this is worth the wait," he answered.

Although the flame in the coal fire on my hearth was low, he breathed upon it and my little copper pot, tarnished with thick patina, seemed to glow red with the water.

"Chocolate is best in the winter's night, when the Moon is new and the Sun far away, but the mountain's night is bracing enough," he said. "You must have had chocolate in Hagen."

"Rarely. Even then, it was only the thin stuff the librarians meted out to us when we had passed an exam,"

"Well that is a shame. We must first mix it with water, and then milk and cream. That is the best way."

He stirred the dark chocolate with careful, slow movements and smiled at me when he mixed in honey.

"Pity this is only our mountain honey," he said.

"Why? I think it is quite good. It is one of the few things I find that the mountains do well."

"Oh yes, the wildflowers are sweet, and were I somewhere else I would pity the honey of that land. But just now I wished the bees had gathered the amber upon rosemary."

"Rosemary?"

"For remembrance of the sea." He smiled at me then, as though he knew where I wished to be, and somehow included himself there, upon a shore at night when the ocean speaks through the tide.

I blushed and looked down at my hands. Even they seemed to blush—yes, even my purple right hand—and I hid them in a fold of my dress.

"Do not hide your hands, Ms. Ludenow, for they are quite beautiful. I especially like your purple hand."

"You must have seen others in your travels."

"I have, but none that wear the stain as well as yours."

The stars rekindled outside and the nightingales sang as he poured the milk into the chocolate.

"Well, tell me, Ms. Ludenow. Is it acceptable? At least a little better than your exam rewards?"

"This chocolate is wonderful. It is like a thick river, of—" I began, but stopped. I did not wish to sound foolish.

"Of what?"

"Velvet: felt not seen in the blackness."

"That is exactly what it is: 'a velvet felt not seen in the blackness.' You sound like a poet. Do you write any of it down?"

"I write the words of other people."

"A pity. You do not have to do so tonight because in my lateness I have unintentionally allowed you that freedom. I am sure you have traveled much further than I in your dreams. Tell me."

We spoke the earth into languages, lands bound by rivers, the watersheds of mountains, and the expanse of the Moon-drawn sea. On such an earth, the smallest shared preference was not trivial, but pregnant with destiny. How else to describe the joy of Aldebaran above the groves of orange and apricot? How else to feel the bass scud of Vatnajökull across the blue slumbers of dreams?

"I am sorry I missed Mr. Dörscher. Did he come by?"

"No, I only had one visitor, a mother who wanted a letter written."

"Ah, well I am glad I did not inconvenience him. I would be annoyed at his dismissal of my request, but your company is more agreeable. Nevertheless, I am afraid I must speak with him and prepare a contract."

"It is a very gracious thing. To come and stay."

"Oh, but you have been gracious for forgiving my lateness. I will come again, soon, and I shall bring him with me."

No, I wished. Would Willi Dörscher enjoy talk of figs and wine in Jerez? What would Willi Dörscher make of the sea around Mallorca?

"I am afraid I must be going." He said.

"Why afraid?" I asked.

"It is an expression, one you use, you know."

"I do not."

"Then perhaps you are not afraid."

The Smell of Change

"So he came and then he left you alone." The troll crosses his legs and then gracefully sits down, like he is a dancer, and yet I can see that no hard rehearsal, no falls have led to this physical knowledge for him. He simply sits.

The light of the stars comes through the broken roof and I mark their progress. Like all starlight, I know it is very old and yet the span of my own forgotten daylight seems vast: my fog, the light of the Sun on the snow. I cannot see those everydays so easily, and the starlight glints off the troll's swimming, as yet unformed eyes. His hair again extends out and goes around my waist, tenderly, yet I can feel the sleeping strength, the nascent hunger of his embrace, and it is there in his hand which takes mine.

"Sit," he says. "Relax, I don't want you to be tough and fibrous from standing all night."

"I'm tough and fibrous all the same; one night of sitting will not undo the travels and clamberings I have done. But I appreciate your courtesy, Anton. Thank you; I will sit."

"I like the touch of your voice. It has a good sound to it. It is deep and strong, but not like the males of your kind. Perhaps this man liked your voice as well."

"Perhaps, and it was pleasant to hear his voice in the cabin."

"Why?"

"I had been alone for so long."

"It seems that so many of you are alone, yet I know many of you are crowded as well."

"Crowded?"

"I think that is the word. There are many of you in one place."

"That is a city," I say.

"I am not sure we are talking about the same thing."

"A city is where many people live, but most of us are alone in them."

"No. I mean the place where there are many you's. It is a place underneath your crunchy skulls and soft brains. It is in the memories of your blood and muscle."

"Ah, you mean the many I's I have been. And the many I's I am."

"Yes, this young woman drinking chocolate with a handsome man is one of them," He stops and flicks his tongue out in the air. It has three fleshy clubs at the end. Even in the dim starlight, I see they are pink and moist. They swell with blood and grow turgid for a moment. But like a meatflower, they fold up into themselves and his tongue shoots back like a frog's. He does not touch me, yet I feel the slather of that tongue is all over me, not merely on my skin, not my vagina, but into the chamber of my heart, the lobes of my liver. He caresses the back of each eyeball.

"And there is a young girl who lived in a city where she was lonely. I can smell it in your body. You were alone in your city and you wanted to find someone. Something drove you out and then this man found you. Or did you find him?"

"Finding usually means looking for something and I was not looking for anything."

"Oh, but you wanted something, deep in your body, your being, you needed something. I can smell it when you speak of this man. You wanted him physically. I can taste it. You needed him."

I do not know what to say. My brain is rasped by that tongue.

"Anton, there were many days in which I did the same thing. Even my anticipation and hope for change was a familiar habit. Like any clothes, a habit may change slightly, invoked by the shift of seasons and weather. It is easy to cast doubt on that life, to say that it was all sleep and illusion, to accept that mindless constancy of being. It is easy to compress time when nothing changes. We take as a matter of course a sentence like 'For many days I wrote out orders' and yet every order was unique. My natural inclination was to simply fall forward through my life. Yet on the next day I stopped falling. I landed on the floor of the cabin. I had needed a change.

"The next day was bright and sunny again. In that way it was no different than before but for one change: my old boots. I often wear boots because my feet are long and boots are comfortable and protective: good for long walks and journeys. Along with my height and a pair of trousers, I have found they give me the illusion of masculinity which is also an advantage while traveling, but that morning, as they stood on the beaten-earth floor, they appeared suddenly scuffed, decrepit, thick-soled. Not much for dancing."

Shoes

The morning after he had come with his chocolate, I frowned at my boots. They did not improve when I put them on, but only seemed to grow onto my feet like old hooves. I wanted shoes. Perhaps red and pointed, and spangled with silver beads: the kind of shoes the thick-calved girls of money wore when they danced around the village fire. They wore dancing shoes—shoes for the night—shoes tuned to a music of beauty I had never performed.

I took out my money and looked at it and realized I did not know anything about Modran Modral.

If I purchased my way back to a city, I could find a score of men like him.

No, I would not.

I thought of putting the money back away, but I looked out my open window, for the day was bright and sunny. The month of May strongly recommended new shoes. I counted out a few coins, and put the rest away.

Benjamin ben Aaron's shop lay on an inner frontier of the town, just past richer businesses. I had notarized the odd business-note or contract for him, but we knew each other through a more friendly and passionate rivalry, for he was one of the few people who regularly beat me to the traveling bookseller's stall when they came for the summer fair. He snatched up most of the better periodicals, travel books of new discoveries in the far western continents, astronomical treatises, and other arcane volumes, but Benjamin was generous and usually let me borrow his books once he was finished. I still subscribed to the *Hagen Freeman* and *Shipper's Report,* newspapers which together gave a wide view of my old city, and I exchanged them for peeks at the tractates, or books on magic he sometimes found. So I put a copy of February's *Hagen Freeman* in my bag as an offering.

His half-timbered shop and house was a cluttered hive of leather. It smelled thick, warm and well-polished. He sat near the only window for the light, stitching together a pair of men's shoes.

"Ada! How delightful to see you." He rose and wiped his hands on his apron, approached me, and shook my hand with the vigor of a lonely man. He was married, to a Harz woman not of his religion, but she cooked well and was kind but illiterate. Heidi tended to his hearth and their daughter, and I could imagine her drifting off in the strange words and languages he would read to her by the coal fire in winter.

"Benjamin."

"Have you come for a book? I have a very nice copy of Fruchwalter's *Waterpeoples*, if you wish to look at it. I don't think I will get to it for a while."

"I am actually coming with custom, and perhaps to exchange this for a *Lübecker Hansaman* if you have any recent copies." I laid the *Freeman* down on his shop table and tried to smile.

I did not ever feel much like smiling in the town. As I have said, I was not like most of the people there and many of them seemed to fear me. It is difficult to return a sneer, save by looking down at one's feet, and I was only too aware of how long and ugly mine were.

He reached up, as he always did, and touched my chin. I looked in his warm brown eyes. "Welcome to my house and my business, Ada. Please, we are friends. When are you ever going to learn to smile? I think you knew how once. Let me see, I wonder if I have any sort of book of instruction for that. It's a spring day and a pretty girl like you should be smiling."

"You are flattering me, for I am neither pretty nor a girl anymore, but today is pleasant and I want some new shoes, so I will indulge your charity."

"Fah. Well, not 'fah' on the shoes of course. It is about time. I made those boots well, but do you not wear anything else? Even just your own feet?"

"I am not like these mountain women with their calloused rock hopper hooves. I do not go barefoot. Allow me that dignity from where I was from."

"Ah, but you should feel the grass, such as we have here, on your toes once in a while. While I should not say this, professional interest, you understand, I will tell you a secret that it is not always good to wear shoes. You need to touch the earth." There was a kettle of good tea on his stove and he poured two glasses. "Perhaps even a pair of sandals? You have such long and pretty feet, I am sure your toes would at least accept that compromise." He laughed and sat down.

"Perhaps, but what I would actually like, I don't know." I looked around, hoping to find something on his walls that I could point to. "I don't see what I am looking for."

"Well, your feet are long and thin. As long as most men's feet are here, at any rate. Thin: a challenge, but one I like. Tell me, what do you want to do in them? Don't tell me wear them 'here and there.'"

"What would be good on a boat? What would be good to step out of a carriage perhaps, or walk across the floor of the old Temple in Hagen? What would be good to dance in?"

"Dance?" Benjamin smiled at this. "Well, I like that. I make dancing shoes, sometimes, you know. Let me look at your feet, take those old masterpieces off."

I took off my boots and let him touch my feet and hold the arches in his hand. He measured them, and set them gingerly on the floor.

"Well, there is a new type of shoe. New for here. I am sure the fashion has already raged in Hagen, Köln, or Spandau. But it does seem practical, so that if you were to ever return there, as you should, I think you would blend back into the world in which you belong."

"What is so special about them?"

"They are made for each foot. The right is different from the left. They are not symmetric, they cannot be interchanged. I think this makes perfect sense and see, I have a pair right here. They are very comfortable."

Benjamin pulled aside his apron and robe and there were two shoes, strangely shaped: they mirrored one another.

"Yes, I can see what you are thinking," he said. "But a man or a woman's feet aren't the same and their shoes shouldn't be, either. Anyway, I have some supple dark Tyrian-colored leather. It will match your hand. I am thinking of something simple, but elegant. They need to be cut low to show off the top of your long foot. We'll put tassels on them. Perhaps some red glass beads? They will catch the light that way, but blend into the rest of the leather, like a wink disappears from the face of a pretty girl that leaves you remembering it. A sort of magic, you know. They come with a very steep price but one that is not difficult for you to pay."

"I don't understand—I have money, but I can tell you are playing at some other game."

"You must tell me why you want them."

"I decided it was time for something new. That is all. I wanted to feel…"

"Beautiful. Shoes don't make a woman beautiful, Ada. They only compliment what is already there. But it is already there. I know that. There is a man?" He winked.

"I cannot say."

"But you have now. That blush is enough. I'll make sure these shoes will catch his heart, but I'll also make them so you may walk away."

"From him?"

"Not from." He stopped to consider his words. I sipped my tea and looked at him while he pondered.

"I will tell you," he finally said. "They will take you elsewhere. They will be very nice shoes, and will catch strange looks from the people of this place, but you are used to that."

"Yes, of course I am."

"But they are not for here. They are for elsewhere."

Day followed day. Modran left a note on my door while I was away at the office, saying that he was gone to find Willi Dörscher and did not know when he would return. The span of time seems small to me now, but then the hours of the days and nights expanded in all directions like a riotous garden of weeds. There was work at the mining office:

letters, assay reports, contracts for mules, iron and men. I would sometimes dawdle at my desk and think of the color of Modran's eyes, for I was worried that I somehow misremembered them. But they were gray: always they were gray. I wondered about his childhood, and I relished how "yes" would sound coming from his lips, either in the daylight, or in the nighttime as a whisper. Yet then I would debate with myself: was he really interested in a skinny scribner with a long nose who was nearly as tall as he was? I imagined his rejection a hundred times or more.

In the nights of waiting, I imagined Modran and I wandered free of the mountains unto places where men cleaved neither the earth nor each other. I called upon my then-fresh memory and promise of him, feeling his hands upon me, even though the hands were only my own. In the darkness, I did not lie on the pallet beneath the mining company's roof with my feet sticking out into the gloom. Rather, I floated in the perhaps of us, and in that perhaps, the wind and sea carried me to the consummation of myself. I would breathe deeply, after so many shallow breaths, until sleep crept upon me.

It was perhaps only three or four days really that I describe. At the end of them I went back down into the village of Visingotha to get my shoes.

"There was a man here the other day. A strange man. I first saw him in the plaza and I remarked on his shoes, of course. They were fine leather, well crafted. Also modern like these. He was tall, much taller than these blonde hill-folk, and he was well-made. He reminded me of the statues of heroes I have seen. His hair was dark—not black and thick like yours, but speckled and shot through with strands of silver. I later learned it was his tongue that was silver. He must have noticed my shoes as well and found my shop."

"Could he speak many languages?"

"Yes. I believe he is from the Kingdom of France, perhaps. Or lived there for a long time. He said he came from here, which I could believe and not believe, for his speech was different, like a painting that was done by many hands."

"Did he have beautiful hands?"

"Strong and long."

"Did he have a name?"

"He called himself 'Modral' or something like that. You know him? Is he the one for whom you ordered these shoes? You are blushing again, which is a 'yes,' and it is pleasant to see ..." but Benjamin's speech then trailed off, as if a single dark cloud of rain had passed over the Sun. "I thought so. Now please try them on—walk a bit for me."

The shoes were not the pointed, useless things of a princess or banker's mistress, nor were they the lumpy root-shods of a weaver. They were cut low so the arch of my foot protruded, and the leather shone like an amethyst in deep evening. They fit my feet perfectly, each to its own, for my right foot is slightly longer, but I could not tell once the shoes were on. Finely braided tassels of gold and crimson thread bounced near my toes, and the leather was worked over in subtle designs. I stood up and walked about his shop.

"These are not magic shoes that will make me dance until I die, are they?"

"No, they're not that kind of shoe, but do you notice them?"

"No, hardly at all. They are not like clouds, or something silly like that, but more like the sand of a beach. Not dry and yielding, not wet and treacherous, but simply perfect sand for walking."

"Then I have succeeded."

"And these designs: they are strange, but I know them. That seems like a serpent, an old Jormandouroborus weaving around my heel to return, yet he holds a star in his mouth. That is the Mogen David, is it not?"

"They will protect you in Elsewhere."

"There are always warnings and warrantees."

"Yes, but really they are no different from any other shoe in that while they may protect you, you must protect them by watching where you step."

They were perfect. I walked in them from the shop and found such a bounce that I realized a skip had found its way into my stride. I had not done so since I was a little girl, and then I wished to run, as a child does when she cannot abide the walking pace of small legs. Where was I going? Elsewhere. I thought of the apple trees outside of the village: they would be a good first Elsewhere.

The orchard of apple trees was in the last days of bloom. The grass grew long and green, and if I pulled up my dress, I found I could easily hop over the old stone wall of the orchard. And I ran beneath the trees, holding the hem of my dress, the free wind in my black hair, now loose; I ran in the far wide country of six-year-olds

This was no memory of my childhood, for in the city of my birth, there were no apple trees. The street outside our landlord's cellar was paved with flat gray stones, littered with garbage and the shit of horses, dogs, and men, save for when the rains came and washed it all out and down to the Elbe. And so I ran under those apple trees that seemed to grow to the tops of the mountains and touched the soft white thighs of the clouds, but they also bent low and left their petals in my hair. I ran back and forth through the labyrinth of trees. It was a small orchard, but a circle is forever and so I ran until I got a stitch. So I let the shoes walk me under the apple blossoms, so that I could name each tree, know its past: who had been neglected by the thirsty bees and who held gangs of them.

I neither saw him, nor heard him, as though he had walked across the grass in the guise of one with no legs but only the trailing mist of a Jinn's tail. Yet Modran stood there on his tall legs.

"From old tales, I understand your cobblers are often dwarves in disguise. You have bought new shoes; I saw them on the cobbler's table and knew they must be yours. How beautiful you are," he said.

"Herr Modral! You surprise me."

"Please, call me Modran. When was the last time you ran like that, Ada?" He called me by my name—it had never sounded more beautiful. "Since you were a little girl? Come, you must tell me. I have a hamper and some cheese and bread over here. Let us sit and eat."

He gestured over toward a tree. There was a woven hamper, its top open with a loaf of bread and a stoneware jug of wine, all waiting upon a blanket. The wind was neither cool nor hot nor strong. It moved the leaves of the apple trees and they whispered for me to sit down. I stood for a moment, mistrustful as I always was. Why had I not seen him, or the lunch beneath that apple tree? Had I not run through this entire small orchard?

"Where did you come from?" I asked.

"I could ask you the same thing. I just arrived."

"Where do you live?" I asked him.

"I live everywhere, Ada. I am living right here with you,"

he said and smiled.

"I can see conversation with you will need to be specific."

"I must apologize. I did not intend to seem crass or petulant. Or simply rude, if that word can comprehensively describe my playful ways. When I say I live everywhere, I mean it."

"Omnipresently? Then you must be a god—or very tired."

I smiled at him, took his arm, and we sat beneath the apple tree and ate.

"I regret my business has not brought me back here sooner, but tell me," he said, "how you came to be here: so far from that City by the Sea. I have been much intrigued by you since I met you. You are so unlike the people of this place, so beautiful and severe—like a great fir tree amongst the lesser birch."

My back was against both actual and metaphorical trees. This was the first time I had seen him in the broad light, which revealed a glimmer in his clothes. The goat cheese was so white against the fresh piece of bread in my hands and the wine had been the clear green of sunlight through maple leaves. I did not wish to tell him anything of my past, for a great part of my soul wished only to live in the now of that afternoon. Yet Hagen bore upon me, and I remembered the mists coming in off the North Sea, bearing its scent. I remembered dark bread at my mother's table, and not very much of it. I remained silent.

"I'll wager it was Love," he said. "For I can only imagine that god could drive you from the Free and Hanseatic City. Some terrible love. Your first?"

"You guess well."

"I know the hearts of women and men. Yours does not

come from the mold of avarice, which can drive a person into ignominy and shame. Yours was not forged upon the hard anvil of hubris, for you have always been demure. It is a terrible thing you know, for you cast your eyes downward—as though every stranger were a murderer."

"I think it is because I am always looking down at paper and ink."

"Cruel and heartless taskmasters, then. But you are not their slave today. I emancipate you from the paper and the quill. Look at me, Ada."

And I did. He had lain down and looked at me with his gray eyes. They sparkled with the thirst for my story, which none had ever done, save Benjamin or Helga. Yet their eyes had only been friendly, brown, and commiserating. In Modran's eyes I desired the distant sea and the freedom of the evening.

"Yes, I am free of ink and paper today."

"And you are free of that first love."

"You are forward, Herr Modral."

"Forward? I am free here, in this orchard. As you are."

He raised himself upon his elbow, and with his free hand he gently touched my wrist. His caresses became a ladder, and he grazed my arm, traced unseen vines upon the black sleeve. He brushed my shoulder and ran his thumb along my collarbone until he reached my neck. I could only breathe, and even then my voice faltered and he paused to feel the humming of my throat. And I remember how he cupped the back of my head and drew me into his kiss. He was gentle and patient. He paused again and breathed across my lips before kissing me again. And then he whispered:

"Tell me of your road." He kissed me again, then: "Tell me that I may see your beautiful feet upon that road beneath the starlight and the Sun. The past cannot harm you. I shall not let it, Ada."

Another kiss.

"Why do we need my past or any past?" I said, and I kissed his cheek, his brow. "Give me this now, only." And I kissed his lips again.

We did not speak for a long time. We ate, we kissed, and I listened to the wind and the sound of his heart. It beat in slow, strong measure. A thrush sang above us, as though the world had contrived the most beautiful song for us that day.

But slowly, the world came back: Modran laughed.

"Ha, we are not alone. Look, there."

"A man. I believe it's the owner of this orchard," I said.

"Ah, he is big, thick-necked. His jaw was once strong as a young man, you can see that. It was a solid, lean jaw you could run your hand along. But for too long he has enjoyed the rewards of a personal orchard of life. He was not always thick meat fat," Modran said.

"Some are born in rich orchards," I said. "Place a somewhat strong boychild there, with a strength bred in the bone, and life will be easy for him. Relative disasters consist of the occasional worm in an otherwise perfect apple or a broken branch, or worse, a stolen basket of fruit. If he's lucky, he can forget these things as his minions from beyond the orchard come and tend to it: weeding here, pruning there, and keeping the interlopers away. In Septembers they harvest the bounty he feels is his by the ordinations of the Gods. He can even bowl with his peers beneath these trees, and fuck a mistress in a bower of heavy apple-branches. He assumes they bend low to provide shadow and privacy for his Jove-like person. How pleasant it must be. And yet he dreams constantly of thieves: they steal his apples, lead his women's thighs away from him, and spirit the gold coins from his treasury. But the worst thief is Time, for it does not steal but simply is. The rot that starts in one apple does not heed this man's strength. It cares little for his breeding, or the borrowed majesty of his family name born on the backs of frightened people."

Modran looked at me, as though in wonder. After a pause, he asked, "Do you wonder if he or you are the happier?"

"You are here with me," I said. "And perhaps the man and I both possess the freedom of luck, though he does not see it. He can lie to himself about the ferocity of his hard work or the scaffolding of theological justification until the Moon and Sun are swallowed. He and I both know in our dreams that luck has much to do with it."

I looked down at Modran and he was smiling. He asked: "How do you know him?"

"I know of him, and that does not mean I simply know his name and who his family is. I have seen him, heard him, and so know he is Friedrich von Duschter, the local Lord. He comes with a thin smile that hides his outrage at any but himself enjoying this tree and the Sun."

"I shall speak with him then," Modran sat up quickly, and then rose to his full height. The man stopped. He paid no attention to me.

Modran strode towards him and held out his hand. The man did not take it. The men were out of earshot, but they talked and looked skyward, then at me. Von Duschter tried to swell in competition, for Modran was much taller than him. Von Duschter pointed at the apple trees, the sky, and then at me. Modran waved this off and moved close to him. Von Duschter did not move but suddenly seemed to smile.

He laughed then and slapped Modran on the shoulder.

Modran turned and walked back to me.

"It seems we are trespassing."

"What did you say to him?"

"I said it was a good day to enjoy with a beautiful woman beneath a rare clear sky. I apologized and told him that I hoped that we had strayed into such a liaison that he was attending to. Besides, the apples are not even done blossoming yet, so how could we steal them? He said we could remain here, but I somehow do not wish to now."

Von Duschter had walked over to a tree and was making a farcical attempt at studying it so he could watch us. I caught his gaze once and shuddered from it.

"Neither do I," I said. "The light isn't so green anymore. There is a fir tree near my cabin that's green."

"I should very much like to see it, but we must part for a moment, Ada. I must go and try to find Willi Dörscher again. I will come to your cabin later," Modran said, then winked. "Mr. Dörscher will not be coming with me."

The Dawn of Love

"Did he come to you that night?"

"He did."

The troll opens his mouth and the uncoiling tongue searches for me. It comes close to my nose. He asks a silent question and my body gives him the answer.

"So you copulated?"

"That is not the word I was thinking of. We made love."

"I am not sure I *understand* that idea, but I know that you humans seem to make an unholy fuss about rubbing yourselves together, or fucking, or whatever it is you call it."

"How would you know?"

"I have seen you, I have heard you. I am at your keyholes, I am under beds. There are all ways: men and men together on ships, women together in the long winter nights when they think everyone is sleeping, groups of you after the God of Wine has removed your clothes. You all seem to do it all of the time and when you aren't, you are thinking about it, remembering it, or trying to connive your way into doing it. At least the stags and does have the sense to reserve it for one time of the year, but you apes go at it through all the nights of the year."

"It can mean so much more than that."

"How?"

"Are you asking for a riddle within this greater riddle?"

"Did I? Speak it then."

"I am the earth, and love is a day. We begin the day with the dawn of course." The troll furls his tongue. His hair leaves me.

"I do not like the dawn."

"I am not sure I do anymore, Anton. But the Day of Love begins at dawn. What is dawn but a time of beginning and therefore change? Modran's attention to me was like the Sun rising and shining on me alone. The dawn is red and She painted my body with Her fingers. I anticipated delight and desire fulfilled beneath Her rose-petal sky.

"I remember waiting for him. I grew restless at my table-desk and I stood up so quickly that my blood left my head. I drowned in the thin air of the cabin; I gulped at it until I heard a nightingale. So I followed the song of the nightingale outside, where the air became like water and rather than a reed blown and broken in the wind, I swayed in the gentle river of that evening. I kept following the song, walking on the path of stones, turned turquoise in the starlight until I reached the spring-fed pool some way from the cabin. In that time of sapphire, the nightingale stood upon a stone in the pool, and the old twisted fir tree dropped its needles: one, two onto the surface; the ripples invited my counting mind to consider the wave of time and so I became lost in time. I removed my dress: a dress so insubstantial it seemed to be made of mayfly wings. The air was cool upon my breasts, my shoulders, and my hips. I stepped into the pool, and my legs, body, arms, and hair flowed down into its water. In its dialectic of song, the unmoving, ephemeral nightingale asked:

" 'Does the water make the pool or is it merely a scooped-out place? The water assumes boundaries, presses perfectly into them and so shapes itself as a mirror of the sky and earth. Ponder your old philosophies. Who is ephemeral? Is it

I? Is it this rock, or you, naked bather, a woman who never enters the same water twice?' "

"And for the first time, which is always now, the water revealed that the nightingale, the stone, the tree, and I simply were. The horizon of time disappeared into the darkness.

"It is why I did not feel time's return—although I know it did because I found myself waiting.

"The water altered its clarity and I saw marble, marble that had once been armies of swans. Before the Queen of Heaven and Our Father bore our tree-bound bodies on the shores, the earth had been a battleground of swans. The wounds of their wars run in serpentine and chalcedony veins, and to this day swans are vicious creatures. The water seemed to ask:

" 'Shall you carve him from this stone? What if your chisel bites too deep and the ancient fissures break and sunder him? Will you clasp your arms around his wreckage and fall into the furnaces of the earth in hopes of metamorphosis?' "

" 'No, he shall be bronze,' " I whispered.

"The water then revealed me shaping the beeswax of desire and then showed how it poured out of the fired clay of my resolve. When I broke away his mold, he stood, a metal enchantment, distant and young as on the first morning of the earth—as when the bay laurel first held up her green against the sea. And even then, his gaze was there, in the gray waves that broke upon the madness of the shore.

"I lay in the water. I lay in anticipation, for it seemed they were the same thing. I knew these metaphors of stone and metal were old thoughts in the world, and they weren't mine. Like the river of Heraclitus, they flowed through the ghosts of lovers before me and yet the water and the Dawn of Love made them new.

"You speak of dawn, but what of the evening?" the troll asks.

"Evening ends the day, but it's not leftover light, some ragged end of time. Evening is when the darkness seduces the sky, and so Modran stood there at the edge of the pool. He sang in that voice of the first evening, naming the night blossoms, cataloging the stars and how their light kissed my nipples and shoulders; how the Moon polished my hair into jet. I felt like a precious stone discovered in a vast seam of coal.

"I could not wait, nor could he. The furthest destination we suffered was the ferns and grass beside the pool. I called into that evening and shouted prayers to his body to bless me with the agony forever. I blasphemed the gods when he was inside me, and I called down their jealousy, daring them with rude hubrics. He filled me with a blunt gnashing. Though it hurt, like too large of a meal after I had been starving, he could not drive the hunger from my blood. He only made it greater. A voyeur could have counted the times we made love, or the positions in which he took me—above, below, from behind—but now I can neither remember how long his tongue was in my body nor how many times I ate him. And yet we were not consumed. Counting is one of the Sun's many children. I cannot count the taste of his seed nor the press of my lips to his chest, calves, or brow. I remember touching his hair when he lay underneath me. It was like the sky in my fingers and the rich country of his body welcomed me. Naked in that night, we walked back to my cabin, and there, in my too small bed, he held my head in his hands and kissed away the outrage of our love. We slept; we perished as Evening gave way to Night.

The Water

We made love through the shortening nights. In the morning I would leave him sleeping in my bed, and in the evening he would meet me and we'd follow the mountain's paths downward, skirting past the town and into the heart of the Visingthal, where a swift stream ran through thickets of willow, alder, and their attendant privacy. There was often laughter and hard kisses. But our confluence would also grow silent like a great river. I do not remember the days and nights precisely, for they were wonderful and my attentions remained in the presence of our embraces so much that they have become indelible and unified.

But as time is fluid, so it returned in Water.

One night, Modran met me at the pool so we could repeat our first encounter. The night was warm, I remember, so after, we lay on the grass. He fell asleep and I went to bathe myself in the Water.

As I washed his semen from my body, I saw the stars in the Water's reflection, though they suddenly gave way and I saw the slopes of the mountains, as if in daylight. I witnessed the trickling of water as the snow melted—how it seeped through moss, gathering in rivulets until they banded together and roared down the mountain to flow past my body.

It was no daydream. I had been alone and outside for most of my life, even under roofs, and so I was good at daydreaming and I well knew its appearance and forms. The vision was livid, unbidden, and—while fleeting—clear as waking life.

Once, Modran had left on an errand of his business and I returned to the pool, to see if this had been some trick of my mind and the night. But there in the broad daylight, the Water showed me a river, somewhere I had never been. A cormorant with a cord tied around its neck dove into the river for fish. I worried the bird would starve, but then, as I watched, I saw him pop above the waters with others of his kind. A man had tied the cord so the bird would not eat the fish. In the end, they all received their due wages, and the wonder of it was that I knew that I would see this, perhaps before me some day and not upon the surface of the bathing pool.

But soon the Water showed me other visions. Often it was my childhood, and I could see the rain and mud of Hagen, and I felt the darkness of the cellar where I had lived: augmented memories, perhaps, but all the stronger for that. I did not wish to revisit the gloom of those days, and it was easy to close my eyes.

I did not tell Modran of this hydromancy. I was afraid. I

was in love with him, that much I was certain of then. However, the joined circumstance of my ability to see into the Water and his entry into my life did not escape my notice. Even then I was well aware of the ordinary sort of spell that love can wreak upon a person. Not all the council of my soul had been sated with the glamour of Love; a minority party began to murmur and question.

What had happened to me? What was I doing? What was this love?

Toward the end of May when the daylit world began to fold up for sleep, he met me on my way home from the mining office. He was sitting on a rock, whistling. A basket of food for our supper was near him.

"I had a very hot day, chasing Willi Dörscher over these hills. I could not find the man."

"Are you tired?" I asked.

"I believe I am merely dirty. Perhaps a bathe would do us both good."

"Oh, I thought we could walk elsewhere tonight, I wanted to show you the mine."

"Not the pool or valley?"

"You may go to the valley whenever you please," I said, and tried to wink. I was unpracticed at coyness and clumsy at it, but I was in love and flirting was like breathing then.

"Very well. The mine first and then your valley. I haven't seen the mine in years, you know. I'll hardly recognize it, I'm sure. I had meant to go up and take a look, but there is a very distracting woman who lives on the way there." He smiled, and I was glad to not be going to the pool that night. "Do you know much of its history?"

"Not precisely, save from what I've read of it in the

records," I said, "and that, I must confess, was to stave off boredom when I had nothing else to read."

"What did it say?"

"Not much, save that the mine was 'played out' and of no use. Part of it had caved in and killed several miners."

"For they delved too deeply for ore that was fast vanishing no doubt. It is an old story of mines."

"The deeps frighten me. Perhaps that jealous old hole hasn't swallowed enough souls. The darkness there is false, not free and true like the night," I said.

"Well, it is a beautiful dark for thinking, but I like the doorstep place, just inside the cave where we can watch the stars come out before the rest of this valley sees them."

"If they ever look upward, I wonder"

"You are right, of course. Come with me."

Along the way he bade me to leave my shoes at the cabin. "I should hate to see them ruined on such a walk, and I very much wish to see you barefoot."

Silently and carefully we walked up the path. Modran attended to me; he held my hand and kept his own pace slow for my feet were unused to the rock even though it was smooth. I could not guess what was going through his mind, though I tried to search for it. I hoped I was at the center of his concern: that my presence made the view of the valley that much better, as his presence did for me. And yet, bereft of my shoes, I felt the earth whispering to me: that many have gone before me, and many with such thoughts in their heads before the tunnel collapsed, before the lung-disease laid them out in sheets, before they were broken upon the mountain. The whispers sounded uncomfortably like the water, though its visions had always been silent.

We walked past a few old pine and fir trees. Many of

them were dead now, like the men below; they were all knotted roots that had dug deep beneath the thin soil. I saw a rusting mattock with a shattered handle and blunted point, and I could almost hear the profanities and feel the bruises on broken hands the color of sloe, long turned to pulp food for worms.

The old mine lay before us like a wound, scarred over by the short brown and green turf. A breeze came up the mountain and gave a low moaning voice to the mouth of the mine, which drooled out a thin, mineral stream, milky like quartz, yet fouled with the smell of rust and sulfur. The tussock weeds and thin brambles had been eaten by enterprising goats. Despite that, the desolation was a garden—for I was with him.

We stood looking upon the mine, and then at each other for a moment or two. We turned to look upon the valley as the light was failing and saw a mist rising swiftly up the slopes. It happened sometimes. I was so used to queer weather in the mountains that a sudden fog was no cause for alarm. Modran took me in his arms as it enveloped us and I did not notice the chill upon my bare feet; I only felt loved at that moment. I smiled and kissed him.

"I do not ever remember it being this beautiful here," I said.

"Really? You are beautiful, Ada. I should think it a mirror."

"You are beautiful, Modran," I said, turning to look upon the old, gaping mine. I thought the fog would obscure it all, but suddenly I saw the postern timbers grow brown then leaved, branched, alive. And the grass grew like waves rushing up to the mine: undulating, moving beneath a Sun I could not feel. And so with the silence of a crash that never was—made up of all the mattock strikes and shouts of men unmade—the mine disappeared into a plain hollow. Sheep walked down into it and the rain fell upon the grass.

"Is this the ghost of the mine?" I asked. I am not sure I asked Modran or the wind.

"What?"

"Nothing. I thought, for a moment, how it must have looked before."

"And shall again someday."

The voice of the mountain then whispered to me: "What is always hiding beneath the green and pleasant earth you have known or dreamed? The guns and coins in sampo folds of stone?"

It was as clear as if Modran had uttered the words. I looked up to his fine face in profile. He was silent, beaming, and full of love for this place.

I looked about me and saw the first spirits as the fog coalesced into shapes: men colored in sulfur, a jaundiced tint—perfect for the wan and filtered light of an angry Sun. They transmuted into gray and granite markers, tomb stones borne upon the earth, with remnants of their legs, their beards like mists, their backs bent over as though bearing great weight. I saw a stream of miners with wrought faces and tired eyes, move before us.

I breathed deeply, trying to remain strong, but I gripped Modran's hand all the tighter. He simply laughed and began to whistle his old song. It was the song he whistled on the first night I met him on the mountain and the setting Sun broke through clouds. The spirit-miners vanished. All was as it was before.

I have spoken ill of the miners in the past, for they kept to the earth and their own company and did not trust me or like me. Yet I still felt sad for the brief sight I had of their ghosts.

Modran and I sat upon some old and broken stones. The basket of supper was nearby but neither of us touched it. My heart kicked against my lungs and ribs, feeling as though it had grown thick arms, constrictors on my breath.

"You're not hungry?" he asked.

"No. Not at this moment. I don't know how I feel. Nor how I should feel here. This place is unquiet. Even though the only sounds are the voice of this mine and you, this feels so different from the valley, from the stream and thickets there."

"Have you not always been looking away from them Ada? Into sights and adventures? Yet always alone? You don't have to be alone."

"No?"

"No. Here, drink some of this wine. Your feet do look beautiful, even without those shoes, skillfully though your friend Benjamin made them."

He handed me a cup of wine and I looked into it, wondering what it would tell me. But I noticed nothing. I wanted it to tell me the future, for I was afraid to hear of it from Modran.

"Ada, I do not pretend to understand the augury of the skies or the gods, but I know that we were meant to be together—that my business brought me back to the mountains just when you were here, that I would meet you."

I was silent at this, for the open space and his attention upon me were so strong, and yet I felt distant from them. The mountain made me sad, for I understood how it had been used. It seemed then a place for the old tales of Fafnir: how he lived in such a hole as this, slowly turning into a miserable dragon. I had no doubt of the truth of it, for ever does avarice—twisted and dwarved, snake-skinned and changing all the time—consume life in such places. Those it does not consume, it poisons.

"Is this ground poisoned forever?" I asked him.

He was silent for a while. "The poisons of the mines are stronger here. Down below, you cannot see them. Trout swam here once before the blood of stones, the cinnabar and slag, had fouled the streams."

"Is there Hope?" I asked.

"Only that your employers can exhaust them and that the treasures of the mountains are their curse. Let them wash the cinnabar and arsenic back into the sea where it shall sleep. It is not lost, but waits. This is the true nature of the King Under The Mountain. The ocean whispers him away, but he rests and recomposes within the rivers of stone."

Again, we sat silently for a time. He reached out and held my hand.

"In time, the earth will pour in upon this old wound to heal it over," he said. He described the practical medicine and philosophy of the earth: how it moved and forged the blood and flesh of its being.

"Water is the blood of the earth. That much is simple. It flows without a heart and so it's unbreakable. Stone is the flesh of the earth. It moves, like ours, as red muscle beneath a thin cool skin. They are at war, the blood and the flesh. Countless pains, storms, chants, and dreams reflect this war, this dance. It's why you and I are like a stone vase and the water," he said. "We do not mix, yet I may hold you for a time. Let us not waste it, Ada"

I turned and looked upon his face. He did not seem strikingly handsome or desirable then, but rather he seemed deep and permanent and that man was the one whom I'd been waiting for. Still, how would we grow together? Just as the view from the mountain could pierce far out upon the world, and so be lost in its fog, so was life with him. Why could time not stop, as it had that night when I saw the nightingale upon his stone?

The mine had grown darker and the stars began their profusions, their conversations in the twilight.

"What are you thinking of?" he asked.

"It is nothing, a trifle."

"What, Ada? Tell me. Am I fighting a dragon for you? Or simply fixing a broken viol? The viol is the trickier operation."

"No. I was thinking of two women in a house."

He seemed deflated by this. "You asked me what I was thinking," I said.

"So I did. What does the house look like?"

"The house is built of brick with rough windows fashioned into its walls. The windows allow the sea wind to blow through. The women are sisters. The older one likes to climb to the upper story of this house where she says hello to the Moon, who is always in various states of undress. She spends the month thinking of witty things she wished she had said to the Moon the night before. Until, at last one night, she can complement him in a practiced manner that seems spontaneous. It isn't. She has been thinking about him all month. And for a moment she feels beautiful, bathed in that cool naked light of the Moon until her little red-haired sisters spits and hisses her way into the room.

" 'You are a stupid, ugly bitch,' the younger one says."

" 'No, I am not. I am … ' The elder sister points to the window. But the Moon, as is his custom, is already putting on his clothes and is pursuing the fawning admiration of a dreaming girl in the western lands. The sisters fight at this point, but the red-headed sister bites and pulls hair. She kicks the older sister in the stomach and drags her back downstairs where they both squat in the dripping squalor of the cold brick house.

Modran smiled. "Oh, these sisters are very much taken with the Moon. Is he handsome?"

"Like you," I said. "But this story is not about him. He is always there as he will be tonight."

Modran considered this for a moment. He had a confused, boyish look to him when he thought hard, as though the act was not a very pleasant one. But then something turned in his mind and he smiled at me.

"Well, I think I prefer the Mistress of the Moon. I am sure his light on her black hair is quite beautiful. She needs to learn how to beat up her younger sister and put her in her place. So tell me, Ada. Do you have a sister?"

"No," I lied. He had not understood what I meant.

Truth Has Always Been Far Away

"You have a sister and you didn't answer him with that truth?"

"My sister, like the truth, has always been far away—like him, like most of them, you don't understand."

"Oh, you are being metaphorical again,"

"Yes and no. I do have a sister, Anton, but she does not have red hair and she is not a nasty creature. That sister lives within me alone."

"One of the many you's we have discussed?"

"Yes.

"Yes. My real sister takes after my mother, for she is shorter than I am and has a thelic body that men appreciate. She was never bookish."

"Yet you did not speak of her. You were afraid he would go after her."

"No, not in the vulgar sense you are getting at, but I did not want anything between Modran and myself. The red-haired sister complicated my present at that time, and my real sister had complicated my past, and I had wished to be rid of my past."

"Why?"

"I had left Hagen, as I told you. What was there was there, and that was in the past. Why should I even remember it? And Modran had said the most important thing."

"What most important thing? That you were beautiful. Why did you hunger for that so?"

"That was not the most important thing. It was when he spoke of us being together, for that opened up the vast realm of possibility I had almost forsaken. I did not want anything to break that magic."

"Ah, but you kept that from him. It seems you kept a great many things from him. Is this normal for your kind?"

"Of course it is: in the beginning and in the end. Especially when there is something that makes us strange."

"But you were strangers at first. Is this where the word came from?"

"That is a good way of looking at it, Anton. The strange and wonderful intertwine on the caduceus of the god of Love. He brings a madness; the visions in the water were evidence."

"You do not seem to like the gift of the Water people." Anton shifts toward me. I feel his hair upon my leg again.

"Gift can be a boon and poison, Anton. I didn't know that they saw everything, living in mirrors and meres as they do. I had thought those tales were old and not to be believed. Yet there I was."

"You are often afraid. I can smell the memory of it on you now. That is strange. So many of your years ago... What were you afraid to see? If this man wished to be with you, why be afraid of your sister? Why be afraid of the gift of the Water. I believe you must have peered into water to see. You did not shut your eyes."

"I peered as far as I have told you. At first I saw vistas and distant lands. The cormorant fisherman was the only person I had seen. It was surely an illusion, I thought. I could not understand it; it was thrust upon me."

"I would say that you thrust yourself into the Water."

"That is perhaps true. Perhaps the only thing that is true."

"What do you mean? Surely the Watersight allowed you to understand the world more clearly."

"The Water is not true, although it speaks truly for those who can hear. I still look and my reflection is always upon the surface and as the Was, or the Then, which grows in clarity, I am aware of the lack of lucidity. It is as though the pool grows opaque and the fish and glades of grass, man, mountains, dresses, and caravans all blur and become indistinct. But it could be clear."

Anton's hair stops its attentions and returns to coil around his own body.

"You say he left, which was a relief."

"Of sorts—it was a deferment."

"Of telling him your secrets?"

"Or discovering them. Why should I open a gift, or share it? Especially when everything seemed too perfect? I did not wish to venture into paradise only to see it broken and mined out. I think that is what I was afraid of, no matter what form it took in the Water's images."

"Paradise? Where was that, Ada?"

"To remain in that place, let the days go by, perhaps bear his children."

"Ha! You could've learned to weave cloth, and you would live simply and love one another. It is what many of your kind wish for. A simple life. How could you wish to leave these mountains?"

"That is perceptive, Anton. You must have eaten many such people. The Visingberg had once been an Elsewhere, but I lost sight of it in the fog of my self-concern. It became an Elsewhere when I left, yet since I live in Elsewhere, I never really left these mountains and so I hear them always."

"How can you hear them if they are silent?"

"They are not silent to all. I hear the words, and they often agglutinate into lies: prayers spoken to the wind, to the sky, to the deep places. The words do not always ask for good. Sometimes they are selfish. The mountains do not care. Look at you, child of the mountain. You are indifferent and capricious: little concerned with humanity. At most we are a moist stew of iron and meat."

I pause and rise. I walk to the shattered window, which is beautiful in its fractured torture of starlight. "How cold and terrible are mountains. These are but anthills, you know. I have been to the Himalayas. Yet in all of them, I look down with frost upon the warm naïveté of my old follies and loves. The water grows into ice and clouds through the frozen contempt of time and reason. By themselves, such considerations, such visions, do not bring wisdom. I have never really left the mountains."

"Yet there is much flat land you have crossed. Or are you being metaphorical again?"

"Both, because I remember that spring here. I remember how it came in the wind that spoke through the young fir trees. They conversed in a familiar language and later, it took me many years to learn it was a dialect of the same whisper, like distant cataracts, that I heard from the wind-flattened pines near the sea."

"While I have never left the mountains, I know too that the sea lives within my veins. When I walked among slag heaps and through the smoke of the smelting fires of the Visingberg, I could hear it, but I did not understand it that spring. The broad light of the Sun deceived me with its illusions of love, permanence, and substance.Yet the light could not drive away the speech of the sea. It spoke of Elsewhere, deep in my body. My heart, which knows nothing of light or time, knew this, but it hid in the bone cage of my body. I was afraid to speak of Love; I was afraid of that language. Love was something I was neither good at nor well-practiced at. Dreaming of Elsewhere had been the stock in trade of my heart for a very long time. And there, upon the slopes of the Visingberg, which had once been Elsewhere, I had felt trapped and ultimately nowhere. So to answer your question, I must say, yes, I wished to leave the mountains, and my savior had arrived on the notes of a nightingale's song."

"Always Elsewhere. Well, it is the same for mountains you know, because the sea will wear them down. They return to the sea as well."

"By rivers, by floods. Yes, I know something of the pull of the sea. It was how I realized that the livid bond between myself and the sea explained the waxing of the Water's power of sight."

"I still do not understand what you are speaking about."

"Neither did Modran. But think over your menus, Anton. Did you ever notice a monthly difference in the taste of women?"

"Ah, I taste."

"You mean 'I see.' "

"There is a difference?"

Dinner

The day after the mine, Modran left to "find Willi Dörscher or die." He said this winking, and I thought he was wonderful. And I believe he had not been gone more than an hour when the first stitch cramped my womb. I went to the basin of water on my table to wash my face.

I remember that it had rained that night and so I collected some rainwater. I smiled at the thought of him and the memory of the rain from the night before. When I looked down, the water glazed over in its peculiar way, as though it were flat, skimmed milk and then it slowly became clear, as though the milk were a fog that was burning off and I first recognized trees in the distance. They were long and tall, pointed like green flames, and I realized they were the poplars of Lombardy. The Water's gaze seemed to tumble and fly like a bird over a camp of men until it found what I was sure was the destination of the letter I had written for the soldier's mother. But where was the letter? Was the soldier alive?

I saw a popish priest-soldier. He cracked the seal and

actually began to read the letter. He then turned it over and shrugged. He gave the page, appropriately, to a page. The boy rolled it up and used it to light the candles in the tent that night.

Where was the soldier? The Water revealed that he was busy raping a twelve-year old girl and so the illiterate mother I helped has a grandson she will never know in Italy. But the Water also showed the Swiss halberd that went through the soldier's head as he ran away from a battle. His blood was red like everyone else's: like those he had raped, and those he had slain. The Water grew more sanguine and opaque. I watched long enough to see a pair of hands approaching him. One was empty; the other held the knife for cutting off his ringed finger.

For a week, I was alone. I had to wait. That was the first lesson. When the evening deepened, the pool revealed. I will not say it was illuminating, because insight's light is always temporary: fleeting like the day itself and the light of the Sun. The unlight was more enduring.

It showed me many things and events. But one thing I saw often in the deeps of the pool was a beckoning, open hand: surfacing now, then sinking. It seemed to ask: "What shall you do?" The nightingale returned to the stone and began to sing.

In the song of water and the nightingale I saw the steppes and the gardens of far Khandormand. I saw the strange buildings and parapets of a city built on the vertical, like swallows' nests upon a cliff. I saw more mountains and I sighed, even though I caught sight of red-robed dragon women as they flew over them. There were deserts, the sand dune bedsheets of the gods, wide and rippled, until they fought and loved in sandstorms the size of mountains. The taiga stretched across the surface of the pool. Was my lover hidden there? I searched for him in the endless groves of birch and fir, I searched for him in a land of temples made from the tallest trees on earth: their stained glass cast shades of green beyond the furthest dreams of glaziers.

The elaboration of landscapes gave way to architectures. Labyrinths, unsurprisingly with walls carved from amethysts of suspicion and perceptive opaline halls, all made in the convoluted joinery in the empire of the Mirrormidions. Yet I did not yet see the Water people. I only met one inhabitant in those walls of bone and Water: a woman whose eyes were made of gold. Blind, she asked me:

"Where is the grass that was growing and is the sky still blue? Are the apple and plum trees now transmuted into smoke? The limbs of children become ash? Indigo and a thousand nights?"

I could not answer her, and I grew cold. She wandered off into a land of whiteness, and there upon the ground, I saw a skull. Worms bred within it and upon the limbs of the bones nearby, until it writhed and thrust itself up: a vermianthropus, a giant made of wriggling chaos and maggot-thoughts, themselves incestuous, roiling and moist. It careened and crashed away into the horizon leaving only the open hand of darkness again, yet it too disappeared. The Water then only mirrored the familiar stars above, like any other water in the darkness.

Though I sensed it was dangerous to ask the Water for my future with Modran, I succumbed to the temptation. Yet it would go blank and cold at such requests. In my vanity I concluded that our love was unbound from the tyranny of any sort of destiny. That it was ours to make together.

The Water became less vivid and intrusive in its visions. My flow abated, and Modran returned. The first days of June had passed, and he was excited.

"Well, it's good I caught him before he headed up to further pastures, but I'm afraid he won't be back down to sign any contracts soon. He gave me some useful information though, regarding some of the other connections I might make here. Especially with Von Duschter, our friend from the orchard."

I made a face.

"I am not interested in him, Ada. Only his relatives in Mödeburg who could help us. I shall have to call upon him and make the arrangements. I may have to travel there. But it will have to be tomorrow. You seem to have lost your dress."

"Ah, indeed I have. It seems I am attired for celebration."

The next morning, Modran had kindled a fire and made tea. I could smell them before I awoke, and in my half-sleep I could almost taste the smoke and tea when he slid back into bed. My feet hung off the end, as usual, and I remember rubbing them together, as if they were my hands. My senses were drawn to his fingertips as he made tracings upon my arm and shoulder.

Of all things, that morning was what I had wanted most.

"Do you dream, Ada? I have been watching you now. You are so still. What do you dream of?"

"I shall not say that I do not dream, but I sleep soundlessly. There is no blackness, for the dark shadow of my deep sleep has no color, no shape, no thickness to it. Somehow in my body I know that time passes, but at what speed? I cannot say. For most of the night, I do not usually think nor feel and therefore I do not know if I dream."

"But what of those you can remember?" he asked.

I lazed in my answer, and thought upon the last dream I could remember from sleep.

"They are lost memories placed somewhere in the attic of my soul. They are sable curtains upon stages of anthracite. The actors are all naked, smeared in kohl. When they are clad, they wear black wigs and raven robes. They carry out their dramas and comedies without footlights or lanterns. I suspect the main difference is that the actors, performing animals, and stitched-together gods bump into one another more in the comedies."

"You are a playwright, Ada. Such language. But am I not an actor in your dreams? Where do I wander, I wonder?"

"You wander in the night. You never come early. But you come in my daylight dreams."

"My business today takes me to Von Duschter's," he said, missing my ribald joke. "It will be difficult to get back here early."

"I would just like to see you earlier. We've never had supper here."

"I suppose I should see how you cook," he said.

"As well as I eat," I answered.

"And how so? How did you ever learn? I cannot imagine anything taking you away from your studies."

"I had other responsibilities you know, and cooking for the teachers and librarians was always part of my apprenticeship. Plus, I had all of the great resources of the library at my command, and so I would delve through French and Italian books for sunny food. It was like traveling the world through the books and then bringing the souvenirs out of pan or oven."

"I see. So what are we going to eat?"

"That will be a surprise, but what would you crave?"

"Something simple, I think. The richness of city cuisines is all good in its place, but it means nothing if it is not cooked with love."

"Of that you can be assured."

"Your affection is the only condiment I need. I will be here before the Sun sets, Ada." He kissed me then, and as it always was in those mornings, the kisses traveled down our bodies and we made love. After, I lay there silently, sipping tea from my old earthenware cup and watching him dress, which was always delightful, for he was so careful and strong.

"I cannot wait for tonight, Ada." He kissed me, then rose and went through the door.

"I love you," I said, but he was already out of earshot, moving quickly down the path.

Slapping my purse against my thigh, I heard the silver coins. They seemed happy to be finally doing something, and I was happy, walking down to a half-day of work in my purple shoes. I had, as Benjamin had promised, already gotten used to the odd stares of the people there. I held my head up that day.

I would make a fine trout for him, I decided. Men sometimes came down with trout from the lakes and streams of the mountains, where the mines had not yet pierced the ground.

The day passed like they all did then. I have very little recollection of my daily tasks. One report is very much like the other, save for trivial things like tons and dates, which are life and death for some people. I sat in my appointed chair at the old oak desk in the mining office and listened to Director Schröder enumerate the amount of coal they had gutted from the earth and describe a newly found lode of iron ore. I wrote accurately, swiftly, but my mind remained in my cabin with my man. I wanted to watch him eat my food. I wanted to see the sunset on his hair.

"You seem unusually cheerful today, Miss Ludenow."

"Oh, it's the weather—you know."

"Yes, something like that." Schröder gave me a look. I remember it, for it was subtle and cloaked. His countenance was hiding a smile, a memory of his own young days and love, or so I thought at the time. Or perhaps he finally saw that the scrawny witch was not so ugly after all. Such was the borrowed flattery I conjured.

Later, I walked through the town to Helga's apothecary shop. I wanted a scent for myself.

"Ada, you look radiant," Helga said. She sniffed the air, for she was a sly one with scents. "And I can see why. I can smell the morning on you. So it's true then."

"What's true?"

"That's the tone of a girl in love, so you confirm it. Your expression gives you away. You are looking feline and satisfied with yourself."

"Who told you?"

"I don't really remember. A few people. Bertha, Agna. They said that a very handsome man was making himself a special visitor to the scribner. And I remember him. He asked about you, remember. I can smell that he is a very special visitor."

I was never more proud, nor more deliciously aghast at the lurid suppositions of the villagers. I was finally the subject of gossip, but I still blushed at Helga's perception. I tried to change the subject.

"I have to go the market and get something to eat. Have

you been there yet? Are the anglers there with trout?"

"They have a few left, in barrels. Alive, you know, to keep them fresh. But I'm not interested in fish. Tell me, who is this man?"

"His name is Modran. He's a cheese merchant from Bretagne, but some of his family lives in a nearby valley. Fallen nobility, I think, like my family. He's a great traveler, and wise in the ways of the earth that I would have never guessed from a mere merchant."

"A mere merchant? Hm. He is handsome. I will not ask you if you are happy or not. You are in love, but that's not quite the same thing."

"What do you mean? Of course it is."

"Think about it, Ada. You have told me some of your travails in Hagen, and I know something of what brought you here. It involved a man."

"More than one."

"The last man is always enough."

"I think you're just jealous."

I stopped my mouth at saying that, for my mood had suddenly shifted. How dare she impugn him or my own prudence? But she did not say anything. Her face bore the broken marriage of a smile and frown.

"I'm sorry, Ada. I didn't mean to impugn him," she said, as though she'd read my thoughts. Her mouth now flattened into a single, stern line and I knew that whatever she was going to say was the truth.

"Yes, I know something of men too, and you're my friend. I have not been to visit lately, it's true, save one time. But you were not at home. Perhaps you were out walking the hills with your man. The weather is good for that. I used to do that once, if you can believe it."

"It is I who should be sorry. You know I have been very lonely here."

"I understand that. I just want you to be careful. That is all. Anyway, you did not come to me for trout. What can I do for you to help make this evening special?"

"I wanted something to wear. Not a dress, of course."

"Yes, of what scent were you thinking?"

"I don't know. Something that is not of here. Something of the South. Where it's warm."

"I have a balm of frankincense, orange, and bitter almond. I think it will do very well." She retrieved a plain-looking brown pot and took off the lid. It smelled of the desert at night.

"It's perfect."

"Do you need anything else?"

"What do you mean? I know you. You mean something by that."

"When you make love with this man, I presume you—"

"Oh. That. No. I take care of it. I mean, we shouldn't be having children anytime soon. I see that's what you are driving at!" I laughed, but I flushed.

"Be careful, Ada. That's all I ask. If you do have need of something later, you know I am your friend and while I may listen to gossip—a professional hazard—I do not pass it along. Traveling merchants have a way of traveling, you know. He may not leave you with a child, but he may leave you with something else. Be prudent and be wise. Have you asked yourself what you want?"

"I want to be alone with him."

"How can you be alone if you are with someone else?" she asked, laughing. She took my long hands in hers. "Trying to find yourself through someone else will always leave you outside."

My hearth had never looked so cheery. The pan was on the grate and the little pot hung on its arm above the fire, filled with spring water, young potatoes, and precious salt. In any other time, I would have never eaten the potatoes so young, for I was frugal and would have rather had them grow larger. Yet I was in love—thrift was far away on the other side of the world where it was winter.

The weather was beautiful, for the Sun had the sky to herself that day, and her path across the blue had been both slow and fast. I thought of the world as a globe then, turning like a Yule ornament of the bluest glass, all in the darkness of possibility. How it slowed and sped that certain day. I swept the old planks, wiped and dusted the cabin, and fretted over books and writing. Sometimes I would stop and write a few sentences, but they were disjointed things, like timbers for all the wrong houses brought together, and the carpenters had no plans for how to fit them.

In time, I recognized an old voice singing an old song and smiled because it was my voice and an old song of Hagen, something my mother sang before her mind dappled and the world was uncertain. For a moment, I cherished this, but my mind began to grope for specifics. How old was I when I first heard that tune? When did the measure and lyrics finally find their home in my soul? When did mother sing it? But I found that even my gentle searching was too much for the rust of my memories, and as such they crumbled under my recollection. I looked out the window.

"It is better to simply live now, than remember what is gone," I said to the mountains, and once again in my heart, I stood beautiful and naked, looking out on a peaceful sea at night. The horizon was a line of possibility, remarkably flat and potential, unlike the stony prisons of the hills that were around me. I marked the course of the Sun. She gave me a little time, and so I removed my clothes and went to bathe in the pool.

In the Water, my shadow asked me what I wished for.

"I wish to fall within his life like you, and, just there, across the afternoon of the floor, I'll touch the boards just a little darker, perhaps make gray the white window sill."

My shadow had taken up a posture of akimbo arms that declared frustration and condemnation of the paths of selfish foolery. "I think you wish for his shadow to stain your morning and its floor. Am I not good enough anymore?"

"Can you not show me him?" I asked the Water. My shadow then disappeared and the Water grew opaque, opalescent, and then became a vase of carved quartz upon a table. It held a slim branch of cherry blossoms.

"I pour myself into you," I said to the vision. "I fit you to give life to the cherry blossom branch there."

As the afternoon deepened, ravens came nearby and discussed a feast: some dead thing. Their croaks and conversation, the practicum of eating, settled in, and their hungry speech reminded me that I had supper to cook. I stepped from the pool and spoke a prayer to the Lady: to live and love with Modran until the stars swim beyond the twilight.

He sat in the plain chair across from me and my few precious things to eat. I never ate very well in the mountains beyond what I could sometimes grow in the little garden. I was not a very good gardener, but I had read enough books to remember some things to do, and Helga was helpful in giving me seeds, cuttings, and advice from her own luscious apothecary›s garden.

There were two pewter plates that held fried trout, fat white asparagus, and the new potatoes. I had even made Hagen's old fish sauce, which smelled of onions, wine, horseradish, sour cream, and therefore home. I wanted home so very much that night.

I found myself eating like a wolf, for I had not had such food in a very long time. He poked and nibbled. Then he put down his spoon.

"Speak to me, Ada. Let me hear your words."

"You don't like it."

"No, it's very good, but I ate too much cheese this afternoon. Tasting the merchandise, if you will. Can you forgive me?"

"It's a professional hazard, I suppose," I said, stealing Helga's words.

"But I can never grow sated with your words. I shall always be hungry for them."

"You are very handsome and very flattering. You must have said that before."

"No, you are different. In you I think I've found someone with whom I can truly speak—who will listen to me and understand me—for while your life may have ranged between this obscure mining valley and the streets of Hagen, your soul has long traveled the world, just as I have done."

I blushed, but I also felt small, provincial even, for that truth still seemed to lie under my skin.

"Then what shall we do?" I asked. He was about to return an answer but I added: "No, I mean not only speak here, but where else shall we speak?"

"Ah, I think I understand you. We can speak anywhere.

We can speak amongst the Anischauven in their great halls on the steppes of the western continent. We can speak in Paris, or Novgorod. We can speak in far Cathay, perhaps. Is that what you wish?"

"Yes."

"The question seems to be when. Perhaps soon, for we seem to be of a mind. I would not wish to see you freezing here in the winter. You are long and thin: beautiful and more suited to somewhere warm, or at least a warm hall in Spandau. But come, let us travel in your words. You must have some tale of warm places."

"I have a memory of an old tale, of France, but south of Bretagne. You have probably heard it before," I said. I felt strange. He still hadn't eaten very much of the trout. He drank the wine he brought and folded his hands together. Had he just proposed a life together? It sounded as such to me, but while I had been dreaming of travel with him, of escaping the life of exactly twenty-seven years that had seen only my flight from Hagen, I could not bring myself to believe it. I had long believed in the hostility of the world, and to find a dream with love in it seemed like a rare theft. I feared that I would be punished.

He looked at me and smiled: "Perhaps I have heard it. But you can speak it anew. I trust you."

"Very well," I said.

"In a valley of the Auvergne lived a beautiful woman. One day a kind man came to her, bearing his friend: a serpent as blue as the iridescent mantle of Our Lady. Winter left the valley and the man sang hymns of love and Socrates while the serpent came into her and filled her with chestnuts.

"But the man's followers eventually came in wains and on foot: mudwallowing women and men, pursuing him with their worship, and they made a desert of the woman's valley. They filled it with their filth and love. When the Moon shone full through the cherry blossoms, three men came out of the East to scourge off the man's flesh. The ground drank his blood even while a thrush sang of the peace of the World."

"And so the Mother's son is risen yet again," Modran said. "It is a sad story."

"But she gave birth to chestnuts, and so the trees came into the Auvergne. They shield the grasses with their handed leaves, and shower their white blossoms upon the earth. But the woman is different than I am. I would not let them kill you," I said.

"I would rather be the serpent, filling your belly with chestnuts," he said, winking.

We sat silently for a while and watched each other in the candlelight. It was so different than when we walked upon the hill together, for our glances at each other there seemed wistful. And our silent concourse was so different than when we made love, for our eyes were closed and we saw each other through our hands, our thighs, and our mouths. Yet at that table, we could be man and wife, for any peeping biddy from the village. I imagined one of them, a mixture of all their apple-dried faces, turning away in indignation at our quiet, pleasant scene that spoke of love beyond their comprehension.

"You still have not told me where exactly your home is, my love. I can only imagine you in a grand hall," I said.

"Oh, my ancestral home. I have told you Ada, it is in another vale away to the South."

"You should take me there."

He frowned at this, and he marked my reaction.

"No. Do not trouble yourself with aspersions, for I am

not ashamed of you," he said to reassure me. "What cause would you have for that? Would you rather I tell you the truth?"

"Always."

"My brother and I do not get along very well. This is perfectly natural because he preceded me into the world, and so I do not have any title to the lands, save a useless "Von" that I do not even use."

"But can you not make amends? Surely it has been—"

"—not nearly long enough," he finished for me. "I don't think you would understand. He tried to kill me once when we were boys, and I believe he took another fair crack at it, with an avalanche of all things, when we were younger men. He could have killed himself in the attempt, which is why no one believed me, but he is a lunatic—a wrathful, hateful man. I would rather not take anyone there, especially you. He would hurt you in order to hurt me, I'm sure."

"With violence? It sounds exciting, somewhat." But my joke fell stillborn between us. The wind had changed. The fire had died.

"With violence you cannot understand. It is slow, sapping. He'd drain your soul from you the way a spider drains a fly, and then he would cast the husk at my feet to mock me. He hates my wandering ways; he always hated my winning ways with people and my good looks, for he is like some old creature of the mountains, with a nose that stoops like his shoulders. He has a grizzled beard growing in cowlicks and lumpy, misshapen legs. He is bald of course, cockeyed, hairy arms, hands, knuckles."

"He sounds wild, feral."

"Fecal, more like it. I do not wish to discuss him with you any further. We are not married. You are not to consider him an 'in-law.' As if such a stupid word could hope to paint complexities of my relations. So you can understand, dear Ada, why we shall not visit the 'old family manse' as you would quaintly put it in Hagen."

He dropped his spoon loudly upon the plate and roughly shoved it away. "I don't understand why you all think that horseradish sauce belongs on a fish. Typical of a city that stinks of herring, its greatest export salted cod. This asparagus is overcooked, and I am overdone."

"But."

"Thank you for the meal, Ada. Do not cry. Though it is good that you can cry, I suppose. Shows the depth of feeling that I expect of you."

The chair sounded like a storm ripping a tree from the earth as he stood and shoved it away.

"I asked you not to cry, but you are. What's wrong? If anything you have provoked me."

"I was being playful, I thought you would fancy—"

"I do not. I am in no mood for your sport tonight. I am angry now. Calling up the memory of my brother was not wise. I need some air and starlight."

"I can come with you; I can be silent."

"I doubt that. I shall go."

"Please forgive me."

"Goodnight, Ada."

"Please don't go. Please." But he left, slamming the door.

I did not sleep in my bed that night although I lay in it throughout the night. I remarked that there were many nights, when we had first become lovers, that he had left. There were thousands of nights before that when my bed held me alone, but that was the first night my bed felt truly empty save for one coil of thought: I had not told him what day it was, for I felt too shy and later too afraid. But in the darkness of the cabin, I wanted more than anything to tell him it was the worst birthday of my life.

The City of Idiots

Why was this day so important? Was it because he left you, lurched as you were in love, or was it because it was your birthday? Why are those so important? A tree does not count its rings."

"They mark the passage of time. They are days when we can point at the Sun and know that we were different then. Especially when something like that happens."

"Again, you did not care to tell him. You were afraid of his power over you. With him, you would no longer be alone; like me, you prefer solitude."

Anton smiles, as best he can with a horse's mouth. He settles back upon his haunches, looking extremely pleased with himself.

"You are right, perhaps. That was the first night he did not go inside me and yet he was most intensely inside me."

"That seems to be a contradiction: an is-and-is-not at the same time. Your kind calls them some sort of pox."

"A paradox, but your malapropism, Anton, is very malapropriate. You must imagine my thoughts occupied such a small fraction of the world that night, and yet the expanse of time and space seemed infinite."

"Why?"

"It's why birthdays are important to us. When we're younger, they are points when we can measure the world. That night I measured the infinite abyss of his disregard."

"But that abyss was only in you."

"In all your depredations, consumptions, and digestions, have you not discovered that a woman can be infinite?"

"Are you infinite in care? Infinite in self-deprecation? Infinite in love?" Anton asks.

"All. And infinite in hatred," I answer.

"It tastes the same as love."

"It should. At the risk of being metaphorical, love and hatred are very close to one another."

"You wanted him to hate you because it meant you were in his thoughts, his body."

"Love is a city of idiots, Anton. Have you heard or eaten what passes for wisdom and philosophy there?"

"I only know that many of you wish to emigrate there. Or did you want to run away there? Exile yourself in love as you were exiled in these mountains? It must be a pleasant place to live."

"It's not. When you first arrive, the city of idiots is always in festival. You bury yourself in the fantastic ecstasies of your new city. You mind neither the extravagance of the lodging rates nor the queer speech of the people there. But after the festival, when the streets are littered with filth, the putrid water and the gutter runs with puke and piss, then you have a different sort of knowledge."

"But not wisdom."

"No, not wisdom."

"You say you had twenty-seven turns of the Sun behind you; have you been searching for him ever since? Answer me with truth, if you can. Is this all a lie?"

"A lie? No, though I accused the world of lying to me that night."

"And what did the world say in its defense?"

"You will have to let me continue."

"I think I can speak for the world," Anton says. He rises like a barrister.

"Your heart still beats and you bear love in memories. Is that not where it remains, always? Small wonder that in the deep waters, where desire and memory are but two currents, the dark water covers your sight, and you can only feel it pull you one way, then another. There is the tide in your flesh and the press of expansive depth in your bones. You tumble slowly without the urgent gravity of earth, without the wings of souls and birds."

"That is a very good metaphor, Anton. Perhaps you are more like us than you would prefer to think."

"Don't be insulting," Anton says.

"But you miss an important aspect," I say. "Time marks the difference as the unseen horizon of the deep Water, for I rose through the depths to the flooded stony caverns through hard channels of granite until I came up to the day wherein the Sun rose and so marked time. If I close my eyes to feel the Water again: memory and the desire become the world as it is. And that is why this is not a lie."

"Modran did not return in the following days and I wore a richly carved mask of certainty. Convinced that he did not love me and that I would be alone forever, I considered the gift of his cruelty and his absence. I had known it all my life. I do not remember the day of my birth; who does? Yet somewhere in the memories of our bodies, we remember it as the first parting. There were other abandonments; this brought them all beneath Modran's hand, as though he wrapped them skillfully in the ugliest of paper, wherein small creatures had been crushed flat and desiccated between the coarse fibers.

"The mind is terribly swift. I know this because it can outrun the thunder; it flies at the speed of a hunting swallow. This quickness is why I could not count how many times that night I blamed myself for what had happened. The subjunctive wings of what-ifs went before the tails of blame, but they flew in circles without ceasing. Only the variation of modals indicated their subtle place in the gyre of my heart.

I can repair this separation.

I will remain quiet and let him talk.

I must not bring up his brother again.

I should not cook for him.

I may love him, and I shall unlearn my old ways.

Leaving Visingotha

My solitude remained unbroken for several days save for my situation in the mining office, where I was alone in the company of people who did not care. I did not venture into the village, for I was certain I would be laughed at. I retreated to old habits—the easiest, most familiar friends in such cases. I remained in bed too long and was late to my time at the office.

I did not wish to visit my friends; I had been proud but was now defeated. I was certain their laughter would fit like a comforting shirt of greasy rags. I dare not embarrass myself. Yet I felt my filth. Perhaps it was the Sun; perhaps it was mere optimism. The Water called to me. While my mind was still dusty with doubt, a hope borne of the most naïve magic flashed within my heart. I looked at the light of my hope, not noticing in the shadow of my desire, I would call for him in the Water itself and ask it to show me Modran.

When his name passed my lips and the silent desire of my soul, the pool went blank and only reflected my face. Was I mad? Was this all in my heart? Like a faithful dog, my reason awoke briefly and growled: even if I were in a tranquil madness, I wouldn't really be able to tell, for unreason is what madness is and so in this ontological proof, I was assured that at least I retained reason.

Every day began with sorrow. Every day bore anger for him, but every day eventually gave way to every evening, when I missed him. That is always the problem of the Everyday. The everyday problem that somehow every day I awaken, either from the sleep of night or the sleep that comes in the day, such as when I was hard at my work, writing useless things. Yet I returned to the pool, and there on the stone was the nightingale. The song was sad and it awakened me with a sudden swift angst.

It was then I asked, "Who am I? Am I the same person that fell asleep? For then that would have been a dream." While the actions of the everyday seem the same, my visits to the nightingale became my everynight.

And yet the everyday changed.

I have learned that storms come quickly and without warning in the mountains, for they make their own weather, craft their own designs to blow leaves and snow around at their pleasure—and for ends known only to themselves. We make hasty shelter and hastier plans to escape their deluge. At the end of the week and a day, for I kept strict count, he returned. If this seems abrupt, know that it was. I do not think I would have done as I did had he not returned so swiftly.

"I should have sent word to you, Ada. My dear Ada, I am sorry. I hope to only ask your forgiveness, for I left in anger and then my business called upon me. I was called away to Mödeburg. I had told you that might happen. But I hope the news that I bear will cheer you."

"I do not understand. But I'm sorry if I angered you. I am only angry that you have not given me the chance to say something."

"And it must have killed you. I know you like to speak, my Ada."

He was standing in the sunlight outside of the cabin. His hair shone and I very much wanted to touch him, to feel his hair in my hands again. I did not desire him beyond this: part of me was still angry with him, for being such a hubristic ass, yet that part was small and crowded out by other more forgiving members of the council of my soul.

"Forgive me," he said. "It was not you. I have been troubled, and I unleashed my ill will and displeasures on you, whom have never done anything but given me happiness in this dreadful place. What say you to leaving it?"

"Leaving it? To take a walk, perhaps? We could."

"No, I mean leaving it now, Ada. I am sorry for the swiftness of this reunion, although as I said, my work demands it. Von Duschter, introduced me to an acquaintance in Mödeburg, who has a relative in Spandau. The Graffin von Brandauer represents a concern that desires a large shipment of this valley's cheese, and Von Duschter has graciously given me use of a carriage so that I may carry out the transaction."

"You will be leaving again?"

"Yes, but you must come with me! The Graffin is very good friends with the hallwards of the Emperor. This commission could change our lives."

"Our lives?"

"Yes, you heard me. How long do you wish to live here? I was absent just now for business, but my business will take me away again and again. Do you wish to stay here, or go with me?"

"I—this is so sudden. Modran, I thought you had left me. I struggle with the knowledge that it was a very bad dream, or that I was living in that reality for a week. You are now here, you are handsome, you are beautiful in word and appearance, as always, and now you wish for me to change my life?"

"Do you not wish to change your life?"

"You may think you are only asking me to come with you, but it means much more than that." I turned from him, to look to the ground this time. All I saw were stones and grass. Their shadows were sharp in the sunlight. It all was too much, and yet it was exactly what I wanted; I had long told myself that I detested Visingotha. But its familiar charms, my few friends, the pool, the nightingale, even the cabin suddenly seemed very dear.

"I must leave, Ada. If you do not come with me, I am not sure when I shall come back."

"Then it is an ultimatum."

"It is. But I want you to share your choice with me."

"But I have no time," I said. "I must pack my things."

"Take only what you really need. Do not worry for clothes or such things. I will buy you the fine dresses you deserve to wear once we reach Spandau."

"The road is so long," I said.

"Yes, and I will be on that road. It begins for me at the crossroads outside of town. I will be there with a carriage until the Sun reaches the hills, and then I shall be off. You are free to do as you will, and in respect of that freedom, I will ask you only once again: please come with me. Let us live together."

He strode forward and took me in his arms. He turned my head and deeply kissed me. I forgot everything at that point. My eyes were closed and I did not think of the road nor the mountains nor the plain between them and Spandau. My stomach churned, and I pressed myself against him for a moment or a year, or so it felt.

"I shall await you at the crossroads inn. Until then, my Ada."

I stumbled back into the little cabin. Practicalities, such as what I would say to my employer, what I would do, what I should take crackled and sparked in my mind along with the dreams of making love with Modran in some ferny spot near the road, of seeing the Imperial City, of never returning to Visingotha.

There was so little time. The sun ran for the mountains and without thinking I packed the old rucksack I had brought with me. I put on my boots, but I packed my aubergine-colored shoes and the old fisherman's sweater I had from Hagen. Though I was facing summer, I wanted it with me for it always reminded me of Hagen and my father who wore one just like it. I wrapped up a few quills, and my seal. I removed my cache of money from its hiding place and buried it deep in the bag beneath the only other dress I had and an old linen shift.

My books. I knew what I must do with them, but it was sore to leave them.

"Perhaps I will find them again, somewhere else," I said, for I have always been used to talking to myself. "Such is the nature of good books, and I shall find and read their siblings."

I collected them from my shelf and bound them with a strap. I knew to whom I would give them. I kept one: my old

Harsager Book that I had possessed since Hagen. Containing the great wisdom of the Gods, it was the most common book anyone could have, although I seldom read it anymore: I'd known the verses by heart as a girl and perhaps that is why I had forgotten them.

The Sun continued its run, and I surveyed my eight years of life around me. The little cooking pot: an old dull knife: the desk that was not mine. Little of that place I realized was mine, it had only been use that gave me any sense of property, but the mine owned it all.

"We shall own a house, or maybe just a Roma wagon if necessary, but it will be ours."

The collective ownership struck me with novelty. Such was the whirlwind of feelings I had that I was giddy with the thought of Modran and I as man and wife. If we grew rich, we could have a temple marriage somewhere. There would be children, although I could not yet think of them as people, as mine. They were ciphers, ghosts before bodies, but perfect. I would acquaint myself with them on the journey, I thought.

"No, this is all too quick. This is madness, more than I have ever known," I said to myself. And as usual, I answered:

"But when have I had this gift, this choice offered? By those men in the city of my birth? I was chattel or at most an aggrandizing fuck, a womb for babies and property. To remain there or here would be unwise. What would I do, stay until I am old, childless and spent? If I am lucky I will die in my sleep without debilitation. And then I shall be burned and the stones and mountains and nightingales will no longer remember me."

"Yet how can I be sure I will have this different life if I

leave?" I wondered. "I am not sure, but somehow the Water has given me leave, a letter of mark for the future that I shall go to the places it shows me, and I will see, feel, smell, taste and hear these things."

"But will I do this with Modran?"

"Perhaps, or perhaps not. I simply know this is the chance for escape that I have so long wished for. My life was built for the road or the sea, not for bitter alpine resentments."

At last, I said goodbye to the Cabin. I said it to the Pool and the nightingale waiting for the dark. I said it to the mountain.

The closing of the door, the sound of the gravel under my old boots were the loudest sounds I had ever heard. My hands smelled of soot, for I had burned the loose sheets of words I had written down when I was convinced of Modran's unlove. Yet now that he had returned I did not feel alone and those angry remonstrations, those reminiscences were needless weight. I had left everything of mine once before and I was good at it. My third life was starting and it was a blessing that I had to travel light for the road.

I stopped at the mining office, which had closed for the day. No one was around and yet I still crept into the office and left my sealed letter of resignation on Schröder's desk. The Sun was nearly to the mountain and so I hurried to Helga's.

She was not there, and her shop was shuttered. She was most likely taking her nap, or perhaps tea in the back reaches of the shop, as I knew she did. I thought of her then, of the times we ate and drank and spoke together and I felt my heart sink when I felt the shadow of her house grow upon me, for time is unforgiving.

I went to Benjamin's.

He opened the door. Still in his apron, he held a book in his hand, closed over one finger to mark its place.

"Ada, you are... leaving it would seem?" He did not smile, nor did he frown. He seemed genuinely surprised. "Where are you going?"

"I am going to Spandau with Modran, Benjamin. I do not have very much time. I wanted you to keep my books. I cannot carry them all and I do not know where I will be going."

"Can you come in for a moment? Please, I won't even ask you to sit down. Now what are you doing? You are leaving us, rushing off with this man? I have not seen much of you, although it's true, new love has a way of taking up a person's time."

"It has been rushed, and it is wonderful, and he has asked me to accompany him to Spandau. Von Duschter has set up some sort of business deal for him and we are leaving tonight. I do not know if I will return."

There was a pause. I could not tell if Benjamin was simply thinking over what I had said, or he was coming to his own conclusions. As people are wont in such places, I kept on talking.

"But I want you to have my books. No one else here will want them. And say goodbye to Helga. I will write her a letter: that is something I know how to do."

"You do, Ada. You do. This is wonderful?" His inflection rose, perhaps too much. I said nothing.

"You are afraid, and for reasons I can hear in your voice, but you are not even sure of all the reasons." He paused again and took my hand, my purple hand and ran his fingers over the tattooed swallows. He turned it over and ran his fingers over my palm.

"What do you see?" I asked him.

He looked up at me. "I see a frightened woman, who was once a girl. Sometimes the girl is still there and she is reckless. Sometimes the woman is. She says: 'this is a colossal mistake. He will hurt you like the others have.'

He sat down at his bench. "I don't know what exactly drove you here. In these years I've known you, you hint at things, and I've guessed on my own that it was love. It drives so many young people to do silly things like leave home. Sometimes it drives them to leave many homes. But, as a gift, I'll tell you that's what I saw there, in your purple hand. If I was going to do this properly, I'd read the other, but you are going to be wandering for quite a while before you find your home. And then, as with this one, you won't know you are at home for quite a long time."

"What else?"

"I don't know. I only picked this up from a book. Maybe you'll meet a shaman in Wild Siberia, or one of those Cathay Poets who always seem to know so much. When are you leaving?" he asked.

"Now, I must go. Please Benjamin. Take good care of these. Consider them yours."

"Consider this a very small library. I am only the steward of the books. If you come back, my door is always open."

"Thank you," I said and we were quiet for a moment or two.

"But in case you don't, I have one request for you, Ada. You are going to travel far and wide. I don't know if it will be with this man of yours or not. Probably not."

"How do you know? Have you seen it?"

"No, this is plain old common sense: traveling merchants aren't to be trusted," and he winked. "But anyway, go with God, Ada, and please write all of this down: all of what you see and do. Where you go. For I would very much like to read it in a book someday."

The Mountains to the Plain

Modran was late and all of my hurrying to pack and say goodbye was for naught. It was nearly dusk—though very late, for the Sun was close to the solstice—and I watched the evening deepen into twilight sapphire. I tried to savor the details of this sight, but my mind kept turning to the daylight and the road to Elsewhere that began close by. The evening was warm, and I removed my sleeves to bare my arms for the starlight. I stood there alone, with only my old rucksack for company.

When the carriage finally arrived, I saw that it was far different from the old post wagon that had hauled me up the mountain; the memory of that vehicle was hard boards, cold, and wind. When it rained, the driver threw an old tarred pall over me and the other sacks of things bound for Visingotha. But this carriage was enclosed in black wood, emblazoned with the Von Duschter arms, and it lay suspended on chains from the axels. I had known of these coaches from Hagen when I was younger, for I had seen the rich burgers of the city riding in them. Like theirs, this carriage had upholstered seats of velvet, which was something my body had never known.

Modran's face appeared in one of the windows. His face was grim. I half expected him to look up at the driver and tell him to keep moving. But he didn't and the driver pulled back on the reins.

"Get in, we're late. I'm sorry," Modran said.

"Is anything the matter?"

"No, no, just the usuals of never getting away when one needs to," he said. He did not step out to help me. "Come, we have far to go tonight."

"All the way to Spandau?" I said, hoping he saw my smile in the dark.

"No, of course not. Jorgi here will take us, but he is eager to get this trip over with."

I could not tell if this was true, as he was completely cloaked in black, with a wide traveler's hat that utterly shaded his face. I did not know him—for the servants of Von Duschter rarely left the estate—and I never entered its gates.

"You have brought only the barest minimum? Traveling light? Good," Modran said, holding the door open. Jorgi seemed to have no inclination to descend and help me.

"Do not allow me to keep us," I said, and I picked up my rucksack and handed it to Modran. I climbed into the carriage and immediately the whip cracked over the four black horses. The coach jolted and I fell into Modran's arms. He smiled and then pointed out the window.

"Say goodbye to all of that, Ada."

I held onto him and turned my head to see the last of the mountains: like dark waves beneath the sky.

"Yes. Goodbye to all of that," I said.

"Do you love me?" he asked.

"Yes, Modran."

"We shall be together more than ever and I needed to know that."

"Do you love me?" I asked.

"Of course, I would not have asked you on this journey if I did not, would I?"

"I suppose not." I curled up closer to him.

"Do you wish for anything? You have probably not eaten. There is cheese and wine here. I must sleep. Forgive me, for I am very tired and I promised Jorgi I would spell him later tonight.

I had not noticed I was hungry; I thought myself too full of life, too full of adventure, but I did not wish to refuse his thoughtfulness, so I drank the wine, ate the cheese, and listened to the carriage move through the darkness.

Sleep became a difficult struggle as we careened down the mountain road. Modran and I slumped over one another or tangled our long legs and arms together. But sleep must have come, for I dreamed. I remember the last began as black shapes, man-like: moving. Doors closed. Someone wept. Though I could not hear the weeping clearly, I knew it was my mother.

I was stirred awake by the cessation of movement. The coach was still. I lay curled up in the unworld of half-waking. The footprints of my dream lay more distinct on the sandy beach of my mind, and the Moon could not pull its tide any higher to erase the traces of my sleeping life. The dream spoke of change, of going and leaving—the freights of anticipation: regrets of what was behind. Yet even this interstitial lolling faded as I became aware of a sharp pain down below; I had slept the night without relieving myself. It was then I heard the daylit noises of the horses breathing loudly; they were snorting and eating oats in their nosebags. Through a chink in the curtain, I could see the light of the morning, and I could feel the warm breath of the fields. It was warm, so I removed the blanket. The door to the carriage then opened and there was Modran.

"Good morning," he said.

"Where are we?"

"Not there."

"Modran, I have to go."

"Where? We are already going."

"Out, you know."

"Of course. We have just stopped a moment to fetch water and rest the horses. There is a little tangle of bushes just near the brook. Do not worry. Jorgi is still asleep up top."

I clambered down from the carriage and stood. The Harz Mountains are not that vast, and I knew that in terms of distance, the plain of the Elbe was not very far away from Visingotha. But I was still awed by the wide fields stretching away to the East as far as I could see. A line of beech trees in full leaf marched straight toward the Sun and the horizon that promised forever. Perhaps it was a small counterfeit of perspective hiding the Earth's curve and its vastness. There were no mountains. My world had grown and I smiled. Yet it was a quiet world, and I blushed at making the only sound that morning. In the absence of wind and birds, I sounded like a rain storm.

As I walked back to the carriage, I could see the mountains in the West. They were still close, but far enough

away that I could relish the flat lands.

"Do you know where we are?" Modran sat inside and asked this playfully. He knew that I was lost and out of reckoning, but I was smiling and happy. His joy in my being so made me happier still.

"We are on the plain, and if I look to the East, I don't see a single hill—not even mole-hill, thank the Gods."

"They are behind us, Ada. Do not look, and they will not be there. You sleep almost like a child, hunched upon your side to gather in your long legs."

"I have always been tall. It was the only way I could fit into small beds. And it was always cold."

He looked at me then, and I realized for the first time that something of my childhood had really slipped, a pathway marker in my forest had been cleared of the carefully laid moss I had planted. I had grown up poor. He knew this now. But he did not say anything. "I was often cold. I am too skinny. You know that of course."

He looked at me, thinking hard, and finally: "That can be amended. I think after a couple of children you may fatten out a little. But we would need to be careful."

"How? Why to be careful?"

"We must make sure that you don't return to the nervous habits, the great weights that your mind bears that make you so skinny."

"What weights do I bear? I feel as light as a cloud."

"You can tell me. Perhaps I will see them better in time, know their kind and measure, for surely I can see their effect. Do not frown. It is what makes you beautiful and different from the others."

The others? I thought but did not ask aloud. I laid my head upon his chest. The carriage jolted. As we rolled on the old Askanleben road, I learned we were not going north along the main road to Spandau through Mödeburg.

"That is a way," Modran said, "but it is crowded and slow. Besides, I think you will fancy this wide open land better."

"Are we going to stop at Falkonstein?"

"We will sup there, but we must press on. You are upset?"

"No. It is just that I had heard they had some fine old books and manuscripts in the fortress library there."

"There will be time enough for you to pore over old sheepskin and paper in Spandau. We cannot tarry, so let us just enjoy the road. We shall breakfast in Askanleben, but I am afraid we cannot stay long there at all."

We traveled throughout the day until we reached Falkonstein. The inn was modest, and we ate quickly of a plate of stew, brown bread, and some beer. Of the rest of the town I cannot say much, since we passed by its halls and homes in the darkness and there was not much light left. I remember seeing a black form, which I took to be the castle, but stopping at night was out of the question. Still, I was sad, but did not show it to Modran. He provided other distractions: in the swaying, bucking carriage we made clumsy laughing love, my skirt pulled up, his pants down. Not only was it the first time since we had parted, but it was the first time he finished inside of me. We said nothing afterwards but fell asleep together.

The next morning we reached Askanleben, the first real town I had seen in eight years. It could have been Hagen, Lübeck, or Köln for all I knew. It was laid out like any town that grew from its own soil: uneven roads like roots, houses and halls stuck in places like the rocks and soil. It smelled of horses and people: commerce. There was plenty of good stone there for the Askan castle and the Guild halls, although some of the older ones had half-timbered stories above the ground floors.

We went to eat in the Ratskeller of city hall and Modran was free with his money.

"For all they know we are the Graf and Graffin von Duschter. Let us not disappoint them," Modran said with a wink as he held my arm. For this I even put my hair up.

I ate the best breakfast I think I've ever had: fresh hen's eggs and ham. There was tea and beer and cheese that had followed us from the mountains, but seemed to taste better there on real plates. We finished off breakfast with a wonderful, buttery apple tart.

"No, no, I am afraid we cannot stay," Modran said to our waiter.

"I am sure the Graf Askan would like to extend his hospitality and talk with his daughter." The man said this looking at me from a ludicrously obsequious bow. My eyes grew wide, but Modran, ever collected, was calm.

"We cannot stay. I am sorry."

"He is hunting in the North, but will return tomorrow. I am sure you may stay there."

"Oh, I would like to see my old home again, my love," I said.

"Yes, dear, but we must press on. Think if we are late for the Emperor's gala! But please, send a message to the Graf that we shall stop on our return. Tell my sister-in-law that her Nania has grown a bit thin in the mountains but I am trying to amend that and give her a fine nephew." Modran winked at the waiter as he pushed a whole Hagen Thaler to him for a tip. The man smiled as much as he could at me. I said nothing, but looked down blushing and hoped it was the way a noblewoman would blush.

Jorgi had finished harnessing the fresh horses when we stepped out and into the carriage. Like a shot, we were away.

"Put some speed on them, Jorgi, if you wish to get to Bärenburg before the night!" Modran yelled this out the window, and then turned to me. "It's a good thing the Askans are old Huns like your family, Ada. That could have been close!" he laughed.

"What do you mean?"

"Well, I have met the Graffin von Duschter and she does look somewhat like you."

"Really?"

"Add a gross of pounds on you, and knock off a foot perhaps," he laughed. "But she has black hair as well."

"I don't think the waiter believed you," I said, smiling.

"The Thaler will erase his mind and Askan won't know what he's talking about. Askan is an old drunk and probably won't pay attention. Von Duschter will get a laugh out of it, for he doesn't like his father-in-law all that much."

"You will need to bedizen me with something more suitable if I am to be the Lady von Duschter."

"You are right, my lady."

"A fine dress of silk with a purple hood and a proper hat."

"Absolutely. We will slum it in Bärenburg, but we'll need some sort of costume for this road! Well, perhaps not right now."

The carriage journey was a time of containment in a small moving space, yet I was free from the closed-in mountains, which had been a greater, more static place of containment. I traveled over miles of my heart and leagues of stories I had forgotten from my youth: of Venelova waiting for Orthus who was lost upon the wide seas. I spoke of Hagen's many adventurers who crossed the wide steppes and the Nibelung Brothers riding to Attila's palace across the very watershed we were crossing. I remarked on the swans in their flight and the clouds that set upon their own amorphous tumblings to where the wind would release them. These thoughts and tales I told to Modran. He listened for a time, but often fell asleep, lying on my right, for he said the sunlight troubled him. I relished the light and again removed my sleeves and hoped that the eggshell of my skin, so long hidden in my cabin or the old office would deepen to an aristocratic milk-tea. I closed my eyes and imagined that we would pass through Spandau and then keep going East, past Kiev even, and eventually out to the great wide steppes and taiga where

I would find the lands that the Water had revealed to me. And with my man sleeping next to me, I could remember when I was a small girl and I played upon a carpet that bore the icons of the East. It was only a perhaps then.

"Perhaps we will not go that far, but I am closer than ever before and that is enough, my love," I whispered to him.

The land between Askanleben and Bärenburg was filled with orchards. Modran purchased a bag of cherries from a young girl and gave them to me. I ate them greedily and threw the stones out the window.

"Are you planting a line of trees?"

"Yes, they will always lead back to the mountains and remind me of them."

"You will never return to see the trees? That is most sad, I would say."

"It is not. The mountains will be there. The trees will be a guideway, as sure as these gifts from you are in my heart."

"My poetess. You should write that down."

I had hoped he would blush a little, but he did not. He simply smiled and caressed my face and looked out the window. I loved looking at his profile that way, and looked out to the same view he gazed upon. It was as though the world was young, and I saw the footsteps of the gods of love and forest wandering upon that land, blessing the plums, the apples, and the pears with increase. The earth had been blue-green in the morning, and just to the south, the Saale River wound on its lazy way to the Elbe and the Sea. The horizon was without end for me that day and my life moved with the breezes through copses and over fields.

In the afternoon, we ostensibly stopped so the horses and Jorgi could take a well-deserved rest. But that was not the reason. We were away from any settlement and Modran did not seem so hurried, so we slipped away to make love near a brook.

After, we lay naked in the soft grass, his seed thick between my legs. I listened to the trees, which seemed to speak in the wind.

I silently asked them all if they had ever tasted the air of the sea.

"No, we have not," the trees answered, "yet we are here and well-tended. The dream of the sea is yours, for your roots found that sandy soil when you fell from your mother. Your time with us shall be brief and to the sea you shall return."

"My time among you is short?" I asked.

"Do not worry. Remember the dawn is honey-red, taken from the bees who nursed us in the spring. Noon shall come again today and complete the magic of that shadowless time. When the evening comes we shall praise her and cup the shadows under her breasts. We shall nurse until the purple turns to nourishing black."

"Is that why the soil here is so dark?"

"Mother Night waits and rests in the earth. She does for you as well."

"The Night is beautiful—" I began, but a voice behind me, somewhat sleepy, said, "Your hair is black like hers and as beautiful. You always carry the memory of Night and Her freedom. Who are you talking to? I was asleep."

I looked at Modran, who idly touched the muscles of my arms.

"No one."

"Just the trees?"

"Perhaps."

I glanced over at the cool, slow-moving brown water, then back upon my lover's face.

"Tell me, what do you see in the water?" Modran asked.

"Oh, I don't see anything."

"Yes you do. I have seen you day-dreaming before." He smiled and kissed me, moving down my body. I groaned and thrust up to meet him, but he stopped.

"There is always more, Ada, but tell me: what do you see in the water?"

Did he know? He had said "day-dream"—perhaps that was all. He did not look at me as though I was some horrible gorgon. He smiled, his arousal returning. No secret mattered much to me then, and so I rolled over and crawled up to the stream. It went from a dark mirror of the alder trees and sky into a gray mist and then cleared. I saw Modran in some fine shop, surrounded by fabrics. It was the first time I had seen him in the Water.

"There is muslin, velvet, and embroidered silk," I said. "You're buying me a dress, I think."

"You're lying," he said, laughing.

"No, I'm not just saying this to remind you. There is gold embroidery under your fine hands, bolts and tassels of silk thread. The woman you are speaking with is proud of her work and hungry for your money."

"Where are we then?" I sensed he had moved up behind me.

"I cannot see. Perhaps in Bärenburg, but let me draw back. No, it's a large hall with many stories, the street wide and paved. It's Spandau."

"Wonderful! Amazing!" I felt his hands on my hips and he entered me. I did not look into the Water, for my eyes were closed and my hands tore into the fragrant grass. And I did not care that we had abandoned our previous precautions— I loved to feel him pressed so close inside, to feel him release inside me.

Later, in the carriage, Modran slept like a happy boy, and I could imagine what our children would look like. I hoped the boy would be handsome like Modran. Considering both of our features, I knew they would be tall and elegant. I studied Modran's face and decided that our daughter would be beautiful, with his fine nose and brow. I fell asleep thinking of her running through the fields of her conception.

Night

These journeys of yours seem to be more about time than space—yet your kind always use space-words to describe these travels. 'Life is a journey': how many times I have tasted that notion in your hearts though it seems like a tired nothing you tell yourselves."

"Movement is nothing without time, Anton. Without time, movement is simply going from one place to another, whether in the world of steppes and seas or in the wider distances of the soul. When we are new in the world, movement is all we know: that and hunger. Everything else comes from these two facts. Time and hunger are the first teachers: to desire and reach for nourishment."

"So you travel and hunger to learn time?"

"Yes, even in the smallest of times."

"Perhaps this explains why your words of action are always moving around so much."

"It is called tense."

"Why?"

"Because tension is the energy we crave and our minds try to make sense of it."

"Like how you waited for that man. It was not long."

"To you, no. But to a heart in love, it was an epic."

"Yet when you were with him it was only a moment."

"A small time—like a night."

His hair moves, encircles me again. It coils, wet and strong. He searches me and I cannot resist, cannot show fear, though his nostrils flare wide in the scent of my fear anyway. His hair cradles my head as he reaches out to clasp my waist. He lifts me.

"You have searched for this, Ada. Shall I grow a skin to contain you?"

And so he does. The skin of a man grows in rapid sheaths over his naked meat and he holds me like a child. He smells my body and tries to search my gaze with his own. His eyes change. They are gray and his hair is familiar.

"You said that love is a day, Ada."

"Love is a day, but a day is more than a dance with that necessary old liar we call the Sun."

"Beneath your fear I can smell that you still cherish the memories of that journey: that day beside the brook."

"And so you smell the water and the soil, the stones and the breezes and how alive I was."

"You have only spoken of the dawn and evening of Love. Tell me of the noontide. I have never known it."

"But by that brook, I did not lie in the daylight, though my body was naked to the Sun. I lay in the Night of Love, at its very apogee. As with the Moon, the self hangs upon a minute of forever at midnight. We are without tomorrow and yesterday."

"Does the night color all your memories of contentment?"

"Ah, I feel you kiss my ear with your forked tongue. Your whispers are promises. I look out and see lines bend and make the cursive flow of rivers and the folding thoughts of mountains.

"At Night the world is complete, Anton. The Moon and his field of stars reflect most clearly in the Water. I am in a boat upon that silver sea. The shadows of the trees move over it and yet I see the stars shining in your eyes. The wind blows and we can taste the golden wine of life, yet its color is only clear."

My hands lie open, palms up as if to take the alms of love. I feel his massive hands hold mine. I am floating in the sea of his hair, and the glamour of his being engulfs me. Yet I am ever the Water.

"Do you remember my head upon the pillow of the earth?" he asks.

"Yes, the clouds are reflected in your eyes. They move quickly, faster than above. I study your orogeny; beneath the stones and glaciers, I travel in the mines, the mind of the mountain. How clean you smell. Not like hot water–scoured skin with cinnamon and musk-scented soap. That is only rendered fat and lye. All the retorts and alembics of the alchemists have failed. They oversmell your secret. Their noses are enslaved to the ephemeral scents of precious time: things that disappear in the life-span of violets, roses, sandalwood, and the burnt offering of myrrh. No, you smell of granite, freshly cut by the bladeless knife of glacial water. Shall I search your labyrinths without order?

"It is like the chaos of your desire," he says.

"And who have you immured there? Men, women, children? From their flesh and hopes, do you conceive the manticores, waiting in their carnelian sacs across eons for a birth beneath a desert sun?"

"Where it warms you like a feral cat?" he asks.

"The Sun says 'waterdrink my warmth.' But you are right. I wait and watch her die in the flames of the West. Yes. I crave the expanse of Night where you and I can share a dhow upon the flat Ocean of the South. The Moon returns our prayers by pouring out carets of light upon us, and the horizon is friendly in the long nights. In the water, a lacework of glowing seaworms roil in luminous consideration of the Moon. I know he is the God of Love. Again, he embraces and reveals us upon the boat. The sails and booms look away in modesty when you enter my ghost upon the sea of these memories. Afterward, as we lay upon the deck, I point out the new constellations. I shall name them and the new Gods within the antipodean sky. I feel your muscles and skin against my cheek. To you and the Gods I will tell the old stories too, of the sailor-king and the orange light of his hall when he returned and all was said and conquered. The swallows fly through that hall, for it's a brief warmth in the cold winter day. We do not wish for sleep, only eternity. In the passing of time, I come to know what makes love: how only the mountains can measure it, how only the sea can fathom it.

"Your soul is darker on the waves."

"I shall sleep in your arms."

"And this is the delight of desire?"

"Hung upon midnight."

"For this you have left your friends, your obligations and your home. Do you know where your home is? Is it here? But you run away. Is it easy to run away when you do not know where you are going or where you have been? Is this why you desire the now of my embrace?"

I open my eyes. He has fully taken Modran's shape.

"A wise man, for he was not sure of wisdom, once asked if we can ever step into the same river twice. Anton, while you follow the course and flow of his shape, and so are the same, I am not. This is what I awaken to."

"Do you not wish to make love?"

"I no longer need to, for as you have said, I have been waiting for the darkness. It is in the darkness where I awake. But as with any passage from one world to another, I was not sure. At the time."

He frowns, puts me down, and I stand upon the floor.

Bärenburg

Even though the Sun sank late in the summer night, we arrived in Bärenburg in darkness. Lights in the windows flickered out as we rolled through the deserted streets. We came to a nice-looking inn—large and well-lit, with ground and first floors of stone and two great half-timbered jetty-stories above us.

"Ah, here we are," Modran said. "This is the Franzihof. I know the innkeeper—a good man."

The hall was wide and welcoming with a good fire in the chimney and a large front desk. Beyond the desk was a wide entrance to a tavern out of which came laughter and the sound of viols being played clumsily; the air smelled of tobacco, beer, and men. To the desk's sides, flights of stairs disappeared up into the gloom.

Modran spoke with a man whom I took to be the landlord. It seemed Modran had a pleasant, jocose manner with everyone, and I realized my lover was one of those men who could walk into any town and know at least a dozen people. I wandered off and found another doorway, hidden under the rise of a staircase. I had to duck to look in.

There were books.

It was not a large room, but the three walls I could see were lined with books. Though I apprenticed in the vast Library of Hagen, this library seemed large enough—just as a pond would appear to be an ocean for a thirsty traveler in a desert. I ran my fingers down the spines and read the names of Feunkenschwelter, Eschenbach, and Gropius. There were Greek texts: Sappho, Herodotus, Aeschylus, Thucydides, and even Alexandrian compendiums of Heraclitus and Zeno. These books framed gilt-filigreed volumes of the *The Iliad*, *The Odyssey*, *Thebiad*, *Knossiad* and *Argonautica*. Next to the Greek texts were Sagas, Harsagen Eddas, a Hänisch *Beowulf*, and two different versions of the *Nibelungenlied*. I noticed a complete *Northern Chronicle* by Saxo Germanicus. I was removing the *Friedrich Book* when a voice spoke behind me. So enraptured had I been by real books on real shelves that I had not noticed the older woman sitting by the door in a great leather chair.

"Tall child, you read?" I turned and looked at her. The book was still in my hand. "You handled those like you knew what you were doing," she said.

I blushed and looked at the old floor, which was still earth beaten under hundreds of feet.

"Do not trouble yourself," she said. "They are here for those who wish to read them or just be with them. Look at me, child."

She was a plain woman, perhaps in her late fifties. Her gray and white hair was down and she wore a black and scarlet robe over a thin frame. She stood and moved toward me softly—yet with such purpose that my body suspected her vocation before my mind could.

"Let me see you better. I am afraid I cannot see very well anymore. What is your name?"

"Ada—my name is Ada Ludenow."

"Ada, you are from the North? From Hagen, if I know that sharp mongrel accent? It is many years since I have heard it in the throat of a sister, though."

Her eyes were clouded and yet I could tell she perceived me clearly by some sight I could not understand. I felt her gaze study me: not like the harshness of the Sun, but like the patient light of the Moon.

"Forgive me, Ada. My name is Nona. You may call me that, please. I am the mistress of this inn. I say sister because I can tell the way you approached the books. I did not hear you. Are you a new librarian for the Burg?"

"Oh, no! I am traveling with my ... husband." I turned to replace the book.

"You were a librarian before and—" she took my right hand and held it up close to her eyes. "—and that was before you became a scribner of Hagen. I have seen a purple hand like yours only once."

"I could not finish my apprenticeship. It's a complicated story that is not very interesting."

"I doubt that. I have lived here all my life, so any life that brings a Hagen librarian here, even if she were only an apprentice, must be interesting. I was a librarian for a long time before my eyes failed me and I retreated here to this room. You are staying with us?"

"Yes, for only the night, and then we are traveling tomorrow to Spandau."

"Sit, the men will be at their own conversation and there is luggage to be handled."

"How did you know I was a librarian?"

"I may not be able to see well, but I know where my Greek books are and I could sense that you were reading the titles. Scribners don't usually know Greek."

"I am afraid I don't know it very well anymore. I have not used it much in the past eight years."

We sat in the warm, snug room, which seemed to shrink as we spoke. I learned the books were on a semi-permanent loan.

"No one here reads them much save for scholars, and they know where to find them. When I die, they shall go back to their old home. We are colleagues here, the books and I: in retirement."

I only asked of the books and plied her with questions about them, avoiding her inquiries into my past and my present—yet she was skillful in her questions.

"You are traveling to Spandau with your husband. Travel is best for the young, although you are not quite so young. Suspended, I would say. How many years did you live in the mountains?"

"Too many."

"I see. Well, actually I don't, but I do," she said, laughing. "I hope your husband is a good man. Too often our kind does not find a companion worthy of us, for while we are worthy and sacred, we are also despised, you know."

"It seems that I was ever born for that curious space outside the pasture."

"Outside the pasture?"

"The Children of the Sun—the cows with their big udders are more useful, and therefore more beautiful to the farmer. I sometimes wonder if we are bitches cast out into the darkness."

"You are referring to *Venelova and Orthus*. A curious folk retelling of *The Odyssey*."

"It's my favorite story," I said.

"That explains much then. But which are you? You don't seem like Venelova to me. More like her wandering husband."

Modran walked in. "Ada … oh, I should have known. Hello, Nona. I see you have met Ada," Modran said curtly.

"Modran: you have plucked a sea-poppy in the mountains for your wife." While her words seemed to come in a calm affection, they were a fair cloak of distaste. Modran quickly took my hand.

"I am glad to see you are still alive and doing well here. I would leave you two to talk but we must go to bed. Come, Ada."

"Good night, Mrs. Franzi. Nona. Perhaps we can continue later."

"Perhaps. If you are allowed, I would like that. I must say that the last metaphor you gave me is a strange one. I will say be careful Ada, for while Brother Wolf howls outside the fence, and he is beautiful in his sleek gray coat, his life is a hard one.

In the room, Modran looked past me at the door.

"The old bag has never liked me. Her son took an interest in me years ago."

"And you?"

"I cannot say I was not flattered by him, certainly. Friendship can get like that—especially when one of the members is young and first exploring the world around him."

"Where is he now? What is he doing?"

"The boy is a viol de gamba player. He showed remarkable promise. I encouraged him to pursue this and eventually he left. I wrote a fantasia for him to perform:

'Desire, do not forget me.' And on the strength of the composition and his playing of it, the Duke of Wittenberg retains him. His mother has never forgiven me."

The night was warm. We stood together in the Moonlight, both of us naked, trying to begin the dance of lovers. But it was difficult, as though the music would not start.

"You are troubled, Ada."

"You've been over this road before," I said.

"Of course. I have traveled over many roads. This one to Spandau is well-known to me."

"It is not known to me."

"I know."

"You know? How?"

"You have told me you have never been to Spandau."

"Is Spandau beautiful?" I asked him.

"The city? You have heard of its charms. The architecture is grand and the Emperor makes sure that everything in the central city is clean. The city does sprawl, so there is an element that does not appeal to me. In the poorer sections you will find filth and bitterness."

"You do not like its largesse?"

"It curves along the river and its houses are bulky even though they are fashioned with cunning. One can get lost in the massive sumptuousness of Spandau's baths, markets, plazas: they are all large, and at first you want to grab hold."

"The city? To nestle into her wide bosom?"

He looked out the open window. The air was hot that night. I thought the sweat of my body would arouse him, but his thoughts and hands had grown still.

"Yes, the wide bosom of the city. Ada, you must know that I have been in many cities and will tell you that most capitals or centers of commerce are ultimately the same."

I understood what he meant. I understood my own willing part in this parley; does not the slyest and wiliest of dialecticians profess nearly invincible ignorance? Yet she always knows the answers to the questions she is asking. I felt clever, understanding his riddles, and perhaps that alone diffused my insecurities, my own irrelevance at being one woman of many. I would be the last of many, which is a greater prize, or so I told myself.

I held him closer.

"I think I prefer a thin city to a large one," he said. "A city built on the edge of some fissure or fjord or cliff. The city must look deep within itself in such a place, because the vistas and possibilities around it are vast and ever-present to its people. They know how the weather shifts. It rains a lot there, but the water moves swiftly away. The city is known for its festivals in the darkness, where the stars and bonfires are studied. It welcomes fathers traveling homeward, whether they were born there or landed there like shipwrecked kings."

"This thin city, hugging the cliff ..."

"... is high up in the mountains—and yet the sea searches for it with long arms," he said.

"I wonder if the sea will embrace it in the winter, or shall the water freeze?"

"The mountains that hold the city provide their own hotsprings. It is famous for them. The heat of the water keeps the sea lane open, even in winter. The people bathe and look up to watch the snow fall upon this and every world."

Although we tried, we did not make love. The musicians never could agree upon a tune that night. Perhaps it was the heat. Perhaps it had been the long road and the afternoon performance. The leader could not find his baton. The tone of the horns was flat and discordant. The cat-gut strings were all broken, and no one wished to fix them.

While I had discovered certain powers, necromancy was not one of them; Modran remained soft in my purple hand and I quit trying. The touch of my nipples to his chest felt uncomfortable, not pleasurable. In my temples and neck I became aware of a throbbing exertion of dull, unremarkably—and therefore erotically discouraging—pain. So we went to bed. In unspoken agreement, we rolled away from one another and I could not sleep. In time, a shift of the Moon's light crossed a few floorboards. Modran slept.

I lay awake and thought of roads. I thought of him on his previous travels: a curious metaphor for his lovers, the women and boys he had possessed—moved through. I felt very small in comparison and imagined myself as the thin city he had spoken of. He would not travel any further than that, now, could he?

I stood alone at the window for a while, looking out over the slate roofs of sleeping Bärenburg, How peaceful it looked—yet my mind raced on with uncertainty to Spandau. What was I doing? What were we going to do?

My hesitancy kept me naked in front of that window where I could smell and hear the city: alder smoke and compost, a dog barking, and a chamber pot thrown out somewhere. In all of it I smelled soil beaten bare and hard and a crushed vegetal odor, like a macerated dandelion: the weeds that constantly vied with the roads' travelers for supremacy. The weeds would win, I knew. The earth moved to cover all the roads.

I turned from the window and watched Modran sleep. Why in nearly all the visions of the Water, the far places I saw, which I thought I would see, was he never there? I looked at the ewer of fresh water a maid had left on the table in our room. I thought of looking into it for answers, but I was thirsty and I drank it all.

I only noticed the bedbugs when I awoke. Modran was standing over the bed. His clothes were still off and he was drying himself with a flannel.

"We should never have stayed here. They have eaten you alive and marred your skin," he said.

I felt naked, unlovely before him.

"It's nothing," I said. "A little discomfort is all. It's part of the road; we shall laugh about this later." I smiled.

He frowned. "You will need to bathe at once."

I rolled over and looked out the window. "If I disgust you that much then go ahead; I'll follow in a mail wagon."

"Ada, don't be childish. I have already washed myself. You misunderstand me. We cannot afford to freight unwanted passengers for free." He sat down on the bed and placed his hand on my hip.

"I thought you were revolted," I said. He pulled me over.

"Ada, I shall grow cross if you continue this way. Are you not unhappy with those bites? Come, wash and let us eat." He kissed my forehead and then clothed himself. "Breakfast will be soon, and I must secure our passage."

"They don't seem to have bothered you."

"I am fortunate. I must taste bad to the bugs. Even the mosquitoes and flies leave me alone."

"You are a bit strong for their palates. I can barely stand you," I said, trying to wink.

"Really, am I that bad? Perhaps that's what the flies are saying, but I do not speak their buzzing language."

We fought again over breakfast.

"I have to find a carriage to take us to Spandau. I know of a coach-house here. It won't be as luxurious, I'm afraid, but I will secure it for the both of us."

"I thought you wanted me to look noble on this trip."

"Ada, that was something I told the waiter in Askanleben, and know that I meant it at the time, but I forgot that we must hurry."

"Why?"

"To have a dress made for you? Tailored and fit so it is proper? I am curious; will everything be about you in our life together?"

"But you said—"

"I have explained that. I apologize if you took me seriously, but we don't even have Von Duschter's carriage and we would look ridiculous as noble-people in a common coach. Have you thought of that?"

"No."

"I am not surprised; I believe you've only thought of the dress."

I said nothing. I plunked my spoon down in a dreary bowl of rye porridge.

"And now you are going to be a brat-child. That is such a remarkable improvement over an impudent snob, and you don't even have the entitlement of nobility to act that way. I thought more of you."

"It's somewhat disappointing, you know. I thought maybe you were going to get something as well and we—"

"My clothes embarrass you? That's ridiculous; if anyone should be embarrassed in this situation, it's me. But I am above appearances, Ada. I don't care that you are too thin, that you are too tall and that you dress in the threadbare clothes that mark your profession."

"That was uncalled for; you know I love you. Why are you doing this?"

"I am not doing anything but defending myself. You should be apologizing to me."

"I am sorry then, I meant no disrespect." I wanted to add "you know that," but I had swiftly understood: anything that stunk of presumption on my part would be an injury to him.

He quietly ate a cherry pancake and drank my tea. The time seemed to slow, until finally, after a year or so at the table, he said:

"I will buy you fine dresses in Spandau. There, we shall have the time to do it properly. They will be purple or crimson or whichever color you fancy. Look for rainbows and pick your colors! I will buy you ribbons to match your hair."

"This town is small. You are right. I cannot imagine we would find something to your liking here."

"You understand. Besides, I hoped you would be happy to spend what little time we have in the library. You have wanted a day to explore one of these towns, and I'm sorry our pace was too fast, but you have a little time for today. Besides, it will help us."

"Help us?"

"Well, you must be wondering what we are going to do after I make my commission." He waited for me to say something, and then, idly tearing at some bread, he continued. "I was thinking we should set up a concern. Perhaps selling something. Would you like to know what?"

"Cheese?"

I said this with enough sincere ignorance that he laughed.

"Gods, no. Books, Ada. Books. We could get enough from my commission to sell books."

"In Spandau!" I asked excitedly.

"I am not sure about Spandau. The city is rather large and already has many booksellers. I think we should find somewhere with a need of good booksellers. Perhaps we can publish as well."

"Oh Modran, this is wonderful, I had worried about what we would do. Yes, of course but where, where? That is the question."

"We can travel a bit more and perhaps find out. I am glad the idea pleases you."

"You do not know!"

After breakfast, I took my inkhorn, a quill, and a notebook with me, for I had hoped to make some notes of the books in the library. I wandered through the town, not gaining as many stares as I had expected to, for this was a large town. Their library was near the massive central castle and was built like so many of the other town halls that I barely noticed it. The chief librarian was a man; he was intrigued that a Scribner all the way from Hagen would come there to see the library. I told him I was writing a travel guide to regional libraries in Saxony. It was no lie; it was something I had decided to do just then. We went over his catalogue and discussed Mrs. Franzi a bit, of whom he was very fond.

"She always calls her collection semi-permanent, but we do not care. She is right though. Scholars such as yourself will come, perhaps, but it never feels as though there are as many of you as in the years before. There is not much encouragement to read beyond an account ledger here."

"It is the same in Hagen, I am afraid, but there are more

people there. Still, this is a fine library."

We walked outside and a crowd was gathering near the moat of the castle, which was not very far away.

"What is that?"

"Oh, I think they are throwing a criminal to the bears. There are bears in the moat, you see. It is not a very pleasant sight."

"No it is not. Does it happen often?"

"Any time more than once is often enough."

A man began to scream from the pit. It sickened me to hear it, for while I had seen men killed in Hagen as a child, it was always by hanging. "Why do they not just hang them?"

"It is entertaining for many. In older times, they would throw Christians and idiots in there as well. It's recorded in the town chronicles inside, but I do not recommend it for reading. It is rather barbaric."

I thought about this for a moment. Then there was a loud wet, popping sound. The screaming stopped. There was laughter. I looked at him and said:

"People should read about mere children and innocent relatives being thrown in there or it will happen again." I then saw another man squirming in the arms of two larger men with helmets on. A third stepped up and clubbed the prisoner in the head, not hard enough to kill him, only make him more pliable. My stomach sank and then Modran came walking up to me.

"Feeding the bears, are they? You do not wish to stay here do you? I have found a coach."

"Yes, please. We have many miles to go," I said, and Modran's surprise was genuine and swift, but we left Bärenburg as quickly as we could.

Our mail coach passed through the thinning crowd. I

wondered at our change of vehicle, but there was no post in it and no other passengers. I then spotted Jorgi in the crowd.

"Modran! There he is. Eating a baked apple on a stick of all things! We should stop."

"Damn him."

"We should stop."

"No, we don't have the time. Lazy servants. I should have expected that. He could have driven us all the way, I'm sure, but he's probably got some whore here he wants to spend my money on."

"I thought you said Von Duschter sent him with you."

"He did, but I had to tip him something, Ada."

Kalblizst lay ahead of us, but the road, which had seemed so clean, was now dusty and fouled. I noticed the horseshit and flies, although those things are always on roads. I felt thirsty and sweaty. Modran seemed distant, perhaps even resentful, for he sat across from me in the mail coach, which he had not done before. The mail coach was one reason the road seemed so dreary, for it was a crude wagon that was built on the axels themselves and I felt every hole and rut that afternoon. I suspected that Modran was angry about Jorgi and his lie, but I could not easily tell. I did not wish to rouse Modran's anger and have it displace itself upon me. And yet this was good for I did not find myself wishing to speak for the snapping and popping noise of the man's skull haunted my ears.

Every jolt of the wagon reminded me of the noise, and the swaying made me sick. Eventually I vomited out the window.

Modran was not angry, nor was he helpful. He seemed disdainful, with a mild touch of disgust, as though he were watching someone clean a dirty child's ass. I slumped back into my seat and he handed me a bottle of wine.

"Here, perhaps not the best thing for your stomach, but it will wash the taste out of your mouth."

I shrunk and drank, but I did not feel like thanking him or talking to him. Something inside of me had changed in Bärenburg. I closed my eyes and tried to imagine our bookseller's hall somewhere. Perhaps in one of the Hanseatic Cities on the Coast, perhaps even England or Scotland, but the coach's motion did not relent, nor did my stomach. It was from that unease in my stomach that a thought crawled its way up my body.

Perhaps I was pregnant with his child.

It would explain much. I assured myself it was ridiculously easy to ascribe my ills to pregnancy. I did not know when the nausea of childbearing started for I had possessed little knowledge and less reason to understand the details of the process. I then pictured a calendar in my mind. It was made of star-nets and comets and marked important days as the Moon waxed and waned. By my count, I realized my time would be coming any day now. Perhaps that is it. I pushed down the thought of his child, which was strange. Did I not desire to see our daughter just yesterday?

My life felt compiled of the smallest things mounted upon one another like a golem made of ants trying to dance with me. But my skin felt too tight for the pincher mouths of the antman's body. My head throbbed. My eyeballs crouched back and squirmed in the dull pits of my head. I crossed them several times, for at least the new discomfiture was different. I sweated at the roots of my hair and I was miserable. I had not drunk wine the night before, and yet I could only remember the horrible sickness I felt after I had my tattooing completed when I was younger; they plied me with so much schnapps and opium to dull the pain of the palm needles that I had lost consciousness several times. Although this feeling was a shred of those miserable days, it reminded me enough of them to settle me further into despair.

What if I was pregnant with his child?

The Indigo Man

I had time to think on this for a while, since our sumptuous traveling vessel broke down a league or so outside of Kalblizst. I went barefoot, for I did not wish to ruin my purple shoes on the hard road and it seemed too mild and warm for my boots. I kept to the side of the road, which bothered Modran as we walked into the dusk.

"I wouldn't walk in the middle of the road," I said.

"And slink along in the shadows like you? A robber could easily grab you there. Why don't you walk with me?"

"Because it's dark and hard to see—"

"All the more reason," he said, interrupting me. "You shouldn't sulk over in the weeds as though you'll scuttle off from me." And then, given the fresh distraction he had walked into, I was able to complete my thought.

"The horseshit was what I was afraid of stepping in. There's a lot of it in the middle of the road.

"Yes, well, the horses on this road eat well. Why didn't

you warn me?"

"I tried to."

"Not very hard. You should have said, 'My love, be careful, there is horseshit on this dark road.' Not 'I wouldn't walk there.'"

"I'm sorry."

"No harm. The hazards of the road are often its apples. Ha! I just made that up."

I smiled. My uncle used to say something like that and even then it was as ancient as roads and horses.

I fell again into thought. Though I possessed a rudimentary understanding of childbearing and I knew the baby potentially growing in me was still too small to be felt, the sense of something stirring in my guts was strong. I looked at Modran and considered his joke. I could tolerate his terrible wit passed on to our child. As a quality, it could even become endearing, but what about his unrelenting self-regard? Would that pass down to our child?

Our child: the thought was so preposterous—so breathtakingly possible—that I remained quiet and pored over the various permutations of life extended into the future. There was no water nearby, save for the lazy snake-path of the Saale as it ran to the Elbe, but it was far away in the distance. Bereft of hydromancy, I relied on the more familiar scope of the frightened, associative imagination of a twenty-seven-year-old woman poised between the first flower of womanhood and the slide into spinster's doom. First, there was a contrite cottage with a roaring fire and apple-cheeked children nearby. Modran would be there as well. This veered far over into the dark shadows of a physician's surgery, or the powder-jar treasury of an alchemist. Better the bitter herb than a sharp hook. I then wondered when I should take physic.

Yet I also saw myself keeping the child, holding it against my dry breast while it cried and men spit on me while I sat on a curb begging for pennies for a crust of breast or iron strong enough to drag me and child to the bottom of the Elbe.

No. I reassured myself of something simple at first, like the room I grew up in. A merchant's cellar at first, perhaps, but my child would have a mother and a father and things would not be easy but they would not be the terrors I had been conjuring. In this way, I passed the quiet time on the road. Pity, for I think the evening was quite nice for walking, but I did not know that then. It seemed far to get to bed that night and I was already troubled.

We reached a small postal inn on the outskirts of the small town. For dinner, we ate overcooked sauerkraut and tough pork knuckles with more gristle than meat. I was used to food like this and just put more mustard on the cartilage, but Modran complained loudly until he was given a smoked pork chop instead. It made him more affectionate than the previous night. I wanted to want him, but I could not. I got on my hands and knees, for it was the quickest of our positions. I regretted that as well, for just as I was beginning to lose my worry and enjoy the embrace of my lover at my hips, his rhythm stuttered, he clasped harder, groaned, and was done. He slept soon thereafter.

I did not; I lay awake and did what any reasonable woman would do. I repeated my thoughts from earlier and compounded them by virtue of the imaginative freedom that darkness and the snores of a lover engender.

In the morning, I dreamed that bears with bloody muzzles

sat and waited in their moat. They sighed upon the boredom of their bone-yard, the beaten earth; their filth, once the bodies of men, was strewn about. The faces of the men were there on the ground: mangled, shat out with torn lips and split nostrils. They had been the previous afternoon's feeding. Other men stood above and laughed and pointed. Some pissed into the moat. Others threw roses and the bears smelled them. One of the bears looked upward at the sky and perhaps wondered if it would rain. That would have been different, at least.

"Ada, you are weeping." Modran nudged me awake.

"I dreamt of the bears."

"What bears?"

"Those bears, in the moat. And he was in there, or had been in there, but he is now pieces of himself. They were laughing and pissing and throwing flowers. How sad it must be to have that as one's eternal now. I can only hope they do not understand."

"They are brutes, Ada. Why should such a thing disturb you?"

"Because I had never seen it before."

"You mean in Bärenburg? You are like a child. A very bright child who watches her mother kill a chicken for the first time. You need to get used to it if you are going to live in the world."

"Do you ever see the memory of the dead?"

"Don't we all?" It was a stupid answer, I thought, made more for its dismissive use than any actual deep journey into the well of the world.

"No, you have traveled widely. Known many men and women."

He looked at me coldly: "You should not presume to know what I know. You are intelligent, Ada, but for all your

vaunted philosophy, read from dusty books in Hagen or recollected upon that lonely mountain, you are not wise. It is true, I have seen and tasted many things in this world, but I prefer life—the here and now—and not sentimental despair."

He seemed to want an answer, but I did not give it to

him. I feared he was right, but for the first time I did not wish to fill the glass of his self-regard.

"Very well, if you are going to retreat into feminine silence, then so be it, but I will not oblige your self-righteousness by trying to prove you otherwise."

I do not remember much of the rest of the morning save a resentful breakfast and silent wait for the next mail coach. In the afternoon, I thought that we should walk to the Elbe. It was a pleasant day, but Modran was content to wait.

"I paid for this passage, so we're going to take this passage. What are you doing?"

I had opened a shutter and was looking to where the Saale approached very close to the town. The copses around it looked wild and primordial against the fields. Yet in all that daylight, surrounded by the tilth and culture of that land, they seemed safe as well. I went to the door.

"I'm going for a walk."

"Go, do as you please. A short rest from me and for me from you will do us both good. We have seen much of one another, Ada."

I did not answer him.

He was right of course, I told myself. We had seen too much of one another. We were both wandering spirits—wolves, as Nona had put it, and we needed some time to run. I needed to be away from people! Yes, that was it: a short rest. I had so long been used to solitude that I was not used to a life of travel and its attendant society: so fluid, unpredictable, and demanding. I needed darker trees and waters untouched by keels or washtubs. I thought of my dreams and forecasts of companionship, motherhood, winter mornings with a family, and even standing by his grave as an old woman.

Could any of it be real?

Under the gracious shade, I could hear something. It sounded like water, but I realized it was the wind. I looked into the wood at where the Saale lay and realized I could not ask the Water itself. It never answered questions directly and often it did not seem to even try. It showed me visions that seemed important, but it would have been just as effective if a Song Dynasty poet had walked out of the vacant air and began to explain how to capture a plum blossom.

The stone, the nightingale, the pool, and the fir tree came to my mind like a dream. I did not think of them. They were simply there. But then a stronger presence pressed upon me—the conquering smell of urine—and I was returned to the little beech wood with its unkempt green. It was more than some single creature's piss. It was an assembly of urines kept in close hot quarters until their rotten congress stunk worse than their constituent parties. It pressed through my clothes, it tousled my hair with moist fingers, and it assaulted my nose like a rusty fishhook. Where? The wind sent it everywhere, and in my attempt to avoid it, I found a path through the two eldest beech trees. The Sun showered the clearing with light, and songbirds, perhaps above the strong ammonia, sang all the more. The smell uncoiled a rope of curiosity, and it reached down my spine and tugged at my hips with a deep-bone insistency until I intruded into his kingdom.

The Indigo Man stood in the center of the clearing. Looking away from me, he was bent over his keg and stirred the indigo and I remembered that such blue is fixed with the stale of goats, horses, cows, and men. The wind died and I heard him answer.

He whistled flippering notes, slippering to the Sun,

reaching for acceptance amongst the chirps of the birds.

He did not hear me trespass against him, at first, for I can walk with the old stealth of the silent shelves. I caught a sputtering arpeggio—a high-note whistle—and then, through teeth, a scrap of song in ragged words: unintelligible and muddy. Yet his rhythm was perfect.

When he finished his music, I offered my greeting: a sheepish hello. He turned then, terrible and shattering to both of us. The cataract of the Sun—such light, such a lie of truth—illuminated his mouth, the mauled and broken lute of his joy, and the shredded drum-skin of his face.

He gripped his stirring rod tightly with one hand while the other dangled uselessly; tear-daubed rage and fear struggled on his face. He was a mutilated man who sang a mutilated song, save for when the sovereignty of solitude, and therefore beauty, protected him. My "hello" broke this privacy as surely as if someone had broken his bones and smashed his face.

"Forgive me; I am lost," I said.

"What, who are you? Leave!" He could only look at me with one blue eye, for the other had sunk into his destroyed cheek a long time ago. His voice thrummed and lisped like a child's, as though he had a cold and merely needed soup and bed.

"No, please," I said. "I am lost. Point?" I cast my gaze down hoping to show respect, but he knew I looked away in horror and his rebuke of my assumptions was swift.

"I am no idiot, tall woman. Know that, if you will. I can speak and understand. I am no dog to be given single word commands. Who are you? If you do not answer me I shall kill you."

My words failed me as I breathed in the pisswork

splayed out in deep blue for cloaks, but I knew somehow in the fault-lines of these last words that he lied. Bereft of vicious beauty, he could only be kind. This is how we came to know one another, in a silence as long as the death of mountains.

He was no monster, but only the culmination of mankind.

We sat for a while in the darkness of his trim and neat hut. I marked the darkness and the shadows: his lovers, friends, and protectors.

"I am Ada. I have come down from the Mountains."

"You are not from here. You speak funny. The irony of this world, Ada, Ms. Witch, is that you are beautiful and yet live in loneliness, for I can hear it in your voice and see it in the shadows of your face. You come from the North where you were lonely and you are lonely still and you will be lonely. I know something of it you see. I make indigo and dye cloth and few bother me. Few can stand the stink. It is my shield from the cruelty of eyes such as yours."

"Then we have the darkness and it is bountiful," I said. "We have no need to share it for it's—"

"—infinite in its kindness."

"Yes."

"Was there an Elsewhere, once?" I asked.

"Yes, a place I left. Where they were. Now I am here. With you."

"Tell me."

"I count out the days but they may go on forever. If life is endless then this is all I do. I paint the clothes of men in blue: the deep blue of the night. It smelled foul at first, but I do not smell it, the tang of the urine is as familiar as the green of the trees in summer. I came here to the indifference of that green, and so I hung my life upon them. It is a thin skin, but it was not shed from me but cut, flayed. It is the only rot I smell every day and it does not perish. I have the company of cows and goats, and sometimes the cloth merchant. He is not a handsome man, nor is he blasted like me. He is the only person I see, and yet not all that often. His wife sends baskets of things. They pity me. But what am I to do?

"It seems brave to live every day with such misery," I said.

"Is it? Say not brave, but lucky. Most days I am alone, and I try to avoid the snares of men. But even frontiered and bordered by this reek, they come because I remember them. 'It is the certain beginninglessness of Death!' I yell at them. They are ghosts. We are all ghosts, you know. It is simply the degree of—"

"—transparency? Like the Water?"

"Yes. Out there I wonder if there is unjudging love. Out there is unjudging thirst, unjudging slake. And certainty."

"Certainty?"

"My father was certainty. His beer was certain and so were his fists. I only need to look at myself in the mixing barrel and I see the remains of the daily beatings that broke and rebroke me before I even learned to walk. He broke me the way they break old horses' bones. He broke my cries by smashing my mouth. He gave me this harelip, for I was born without one. But my mouth could still partake of his cup and his curse when I was old enough to run away on withered legs.

"Then I learned the certainty of vomit. I fouled myself in the square for jeers, for laughter and coins. I was ever thirsty for beer and bile. The glee-faces of those men and women were thirsty, watching the vomiting boytroll dance on bandy legs for bad wine.

"And my mother? I hate that bitch, the one that bore me and the one that loved me in the short moments of remembered tenderness but did not bear me far enough away. She did not stand between my father and my face. He broke her and she fled like a shadow in the morning. But one day the Sun did not come to shine on me. The rain came and washed me, lying there on the old stones. A godman came and took pity on me and taught me some letters, taught me the rudiments of this trade. I knew that I was bereft of love out there and so I followed him here, for this was a holy place, he said. I buried him here, and the earth has smoothed so you would never know it. But even here, I drank glasses of desire. I dreamed a face, a beautiful woman's face such as yours.

"No. Do not fear me. I am safe now. Safe from you, because I looked into the river and renounced love. I cursed it and cut myself free from desire. When I cast it into the river, what Goddess sprang from my blood? Freed from thirst, and cauterized from desire, only Memory walked upon the bank, but she is a patchwork giantess made of all the broken times of my life. Memory is the cruelest of Gods. If only I were a wolf, or swallow, like those upon your hand, I would live in the movement of my body, without a past save that which lives sleeping in my blood. To live without a future! But no, we live on seas of memories. I live through every day, for every day passes.

"Forgive me. I sometimes forget memories. It is just your presence. A ghost like all the others that makes me look backward. Know also that the darkness rises with the Moon and I walk with them in the free possibility of the night."

He smiled at this—two teeth in the glowering freedom of his cabin—and I cried.

"You have pierced my webs, Ada, and come to bring me what—your tears?"

"This is the cruelest of my blows," I said.

"Do not weep. Or weep for me, yes, I shall take those tears now as payment long due from the world. Let me gather them, here. I shall keep them vialed as a memory of our meeting. No, do not speak. Only cry, Ada, for there is nothing more I require from you."

And where he touched my face, to gather the tears, he left streaks of indigo until I was smeared in the fragrant abject blue.

When I left I walked in the exile of green. I walked wet with the urine of conventional thought and reassurance. It began with but one common phrase, a line of old verse: "There but for the grace of the Gods go I." Such a lie to keep us safe in the fortress of disregard. What Gods? The Gods of Justice? My unfaith in them had long been confirmed before that glade. The Gods of Power and Strength? What meaning or power is there in crushing an infant's face? The Gods of Cruelty? No, they alone wore the masks of human flesh, and so are nothing but decorations placed upon the implacable meaninglessness of this world. I did not feel better for myself for having met him, for having heard him. There was only the mixed and awful truth of him. Of what men made. I returned to the world of men that I remembered. His face appeared again to me: the protean convolutions of his injuries, his tears from ruined sockets, his mushroom nose, how his broken jaw lay beached between his scarred cheeks. Whale-like was his skin. I had seen whales, for sometimes their corpses were brought back to Hagen. That was a world of men: the world that had dipped into the water with barbed iron and then the stabbing lances to violate and ruin a life.

I sobbed. My eyes felt red, as though the hay fever was thick upon me, and my stomach not only felt empty; no, it also felt as if I had eaten one of those frozen whalebone-traps of the North that unfold in the stomachs of distant white bears. I cried at the thought of my child, perhaps unborn within my womb. She would come into this world to be beaten, raped, and left to die without a care to her name. Worse, she could be hopeful and continue. Better that I should give birth to a sleeping stone.

Rapt in such thoughts, I stumbled to the grass. I lay there for a long time, but in time, I remarked the grass smelled sweet. How? How was the summer sky so blue and how could the ocean's dreams sail so beautifully in thick white clouds across that sky?

What would I say to my lover? Something had shifted, changed. I did not carry his child. Those are the only words I can put to the knowledge I possessed as I crawled to my feet. And my feet knew the way back. I do not know how long it was until I came to the mail-yards. I saw Modran. He was standing near the coach stables. There was a girl there. She was blonde, smiling. Barefoot. A single bare shoulder was revealed by her skewed dress. She playfully slapped at Modran's chin with a single, perfect rose.

Mother Elbe

She was flirting with me,' he said. I did not know what to believe; I could only remain silent, for I wished it to be true. I told myself that I would have to endure such things because he was so lovely, so attractive, so—"

"Wait, stop. This Indigo Man—I have not forgotten him, unlike you, so bound up in suspicion and your own love-madness for this man of yours. Do you expect me to believe an unlettered man, beaten and twisted by the hands of his father, said these things to you?"

"You know the hearts and blood of man, Anton. You can smell his memory on my skin, I am sure. Know that exactly what he said was unimportant; those were the words I heard."

"You mutilated his song with your trespass just as you mutilated my night."

"There is hardly a comparison, Anton. I came here with a purpose: to find my lover."

"To find love?"

"I would think a being of your sagacity would realize that is all quite impossible now."

"How so?"

"Where is the grass that was growing in that orchard where Modran and I ate, all those years ago? A few apple trees may remain if they are lucky. Most are smoke. The indigo of a thousand nights? That is less than three years. That summer with Modran was shorter than the life of a songbird roosting in the apple trees."

"Yet the things you did are still with you. You tell them to me, which indicates an investment of some kind."

"It's called learning, Anton. I think you call it eating."

"All the same."

"No it's not. In the case of learning, the teacher is not always consumed."

"Yet you eat them, sometimes."

"They are consumed by their pupils, their duty. There are many mouths."

"Are you being metaphoric?"

"The end result is the same whether figurative or literal."

"This Indigo Man, was he a teacher? Did you eat him?"

"I could not consume him, Anton. The very feast of his presence overwhelmed my blood, and he gave hard lessons. There he was, alone like some monster—and yet he was a man. Tell me, Anton, are you ever lonely? For your kind? There was once a lonely troll in Denmark."

"Alas, poor Grendel, I knew him: a fellow of infinite hate, of most excellent wrath; he had eaten Danish meat a thousand times."

"Choice words. I have heard them before."

Anton waves this off and continues:

"Grendel's blood ran thick, from the very start, with your kind's red. He had a raw and bloody navel that never closed, you know. That was the sign. And his mother? She never dropped the bloody lacework you are all first blanketed with. So their chord was there, yet not there. Answer me that riddle."

"It is Love, Anton, which is why this was a riddle to which you asked to learn the answer. You do not understand it." He frowns at this, and I continue: "It burrows into our bellies and connects us, even for a few moments, some for a lifetime. It is passion, for as surely as love can beget hatred, passion begets pain. We feel it most intimately when our loved ones hurt."

"Is that why you cry?"

"Yes."

"But you did not even know this indigo man. I believe you only remember him because it is a common thing for your kind to reward themselves through the suffering of others. You said so yourself."

"Yes, Anton, but if you were listening closely, that only began my course of thought. It is a selfish, terrible thing to think of oneself favorably through the pain of others. Yet it is a start: to recognize and know that pain, that misery. Though we cannot walk without our skins as you do, some of us, if luck prevails, learn to be flayed down to our marrow at times like those. I was left with the pain. But know that we can own that pain: one of the few sureties in this world and one I know the Gods do not gladly give us. What we do with that pain is what matters, for it is something your kind can never understand and the greatest deeds of my kind are built upon the iron shoulders of this pain.

Anton says nothing to this, but draws Modran's beautiful

knees up to his chin. I count every toe. I eye the flexing tendon in his legs and his thick, half-turgid cock. I know the hollows in the muscles of his buttocks; they were favorites of mine. His hair, yes, and his ear … I could almost taste the lobe again.

"Can't you change your appearance, please?" I ask.

"Why?"

"I find that particular costume to be distracting."

"That of your naked lover? I would guess its familiarity would be welcome. Oh yes, how sad it must have been for you to find that barn girl tempting him? Yet there you were. Alone in the wide world, as it were, yet you were not alone."

"He said he had done nothing. I had no reason or proof against him."

Anton leans back against the wall, his arms behind his head in casual amusement. He is obviously aroused. He smiles at me. For a moment there is a clamor in the skull parliament. One Ada wishes to mount him. Another Ada wishes to strangle him. Both are young, beautiful, and black-haired. They are strong, but not strong enough.

Anton continues: "And it is a common thing for the women of your kind to forgive. Yet you never forget, do you? You still desire him. Me."

I laugh. As with human men, this deflates him.

"Anton, often when I pleasure myself, I remember him."

"Because you still want him. You want to overpower and conquer him."

"No. For after the release of my pleasure, I lie wherever I am and know that the man in my pleasure is not that man, just as you are not that man."

"Who is he then, a convenient lie?"

"I used to chastise myself in that way, but no. Is my

memory true? Perhaps it is better to say that there is some truth in these sensual dreams, but my heart still does not understand. But you are right. It never forgets, for it does not live in Time. Just as the serenity of the stone, the bird, and pool remain; I do not *remember* the rose and his chin. The rose and his chin *are*. I can feel that languorous tap of hers; he stares at her breasts and I can feel the absence of mine.

"We left the town and went on to Korby, the ferry crossing at the Great Elbe, and there we would wait until the dawn. I could remember her tittering as Modran and I fought in the cramped little inn. "I have you!" I yelled when we fell to angry sex. I did not feel supreme. Anton, it is a curious mix of outrage and shame to hear the laughter of another woman in your mind, even as your lover cleaves into you, clutches at you. He told me he loved me. But they always love you just before they come.

"Modran removed himself from me and was covered in my blood, for my time had come, and I remember what he said then: 'How could you? Why did you not tell me?' I fought with him again, for if I fought with him, I had proof he was there. That much I knew. But when he fell asleep, I stole away from him and wandered to the river. Where would I go? What would I do if he left me by the road? I had nothing save for a few things. Nothing.

"And what did Mother Elbe tell you, Ada? Her waters run through your heart."

I did not seek the River to hear Her tell. The Moon reflected and shivered in Her wide body. I looked at the Moon, with his attendant spider clouds, mischief makers, sycophants. They gossiped auguries but I ignored them.

My loneliness was perfect. My lie lay bare; how much I

wished to be apart from myself, or for my self to be done. Everything was alone. I closed my eyes and whispered a prayer:

"Mother Elbe, we are all rivers, born in forests and mountains. We do not know the flow. We do not know where we shall go save to your dark rolls of sound: each occurrence of our life ripples out until we join the sea and are forgotten. Mother Elbe, where shall I go? What shall I do in this place?"

The River breathed, for Mother Elbe is a Dragon; her breath and dreams are the clouds and fog that remember those plains we cross, the mountains we climb. I had not seen Her since I left my home.

"Are you the same? Your waters are different, as are mine. Am I the same?' I asked.

I wanted her embrace and to never step into the Beyond of Again. But I was afraid of what She would show me before the end: the perhaps, always the tugging worm, naked and blind in the lodes of the earth, dragging me, leaving tunnels of longing that are beautiful and cold, bereft of the life I ran away from. The voice of Mother Elbe came, in rhythm, beyond my fathoming.

Bloody, I waded into Her. I felt naked in the alone, even though I wore my shift. Death would be alone, I told myself. No one will bother me amongst the stone pillars, drowned and forgotten in the depths of my Mother. She drank the blood she gave me and tripped me with a sunken stone. That was when I opened my eyes and saw.

I knew his shape as it was framed in the wooden planks and beams of that cellar in Hagen. I knew his back, his boots. I could feel the curl of his hair and I knew that his gaze was far away. How I hated him. How I loved him. This time would be different. I would stop him. It was then I fell.

Into the River, not arms, but wide black water. His shape became a shadow. The shadow turned in the Water and reached out to me. His hands were strong, grabbed hard in the gravity beyond the earth, and down I went into the River.

Yet quickly, as always, he released me. But down I went, for I would not be abandoned, not again. I would catch him; catch up to him with my skinny legs, my clasping arms. So down I followed him until I could walk after him. Does this sound strange? You know the laws beneath the Water are not the same as in the sun-drenched lie we call the truth of day.

I wandered through the shapeless Waterlands, my time-mind adrift around me. The being who cares only seeks the shadow in the Water, intangible and therefore stronger than any cast on land. I walked into wide spaces, frozen meres of

glass so vast as to be worthless. I walked upon the cold and cutting waves until I reached a shore of iron, rusting and blank, where blind ghosts stood, and the iron men and mermaids of the glass sea considered them to be fantastic folk, elves in their world. The ghosts were women, men, and children from this world. Yet this beach was not desolate but populated by spidery creatures, intricate crustaceans of copper and steel, who dug through piles of rust-shit for kernels of food. Though the spiders perceived the ghosts and hungrily tried to eat their phosphor bones. They passed through the insubstantialities and gnashed against one another in deaf anger. The Indigo Man was the last ghost I saw. He waited on that horrible sand for a ship to come and bring him the cargo of a single unconditioned kiss. And I learned then how much of the world's sorrow swims in the vast ocean of broken, modest dreams.

The storm came from the sea there, as it does here. It brought the rain of unlight, of profound time, and my hair ran in black ink down my face until sight and memory were gone.

"Yet you did not drown," Anton says. "You are here telling me all of this."

"I awoke. I was soaked and tired but sleep had not yet finished with me. Sleep only allowed me one wakeful moment: to witness the Moon setting over the west bank of the Elbe."

From the Elbe to Ravenstein

I stood waiting, wrapped in a ragged blanket some kind soul had thrown over me in the morning. From a distance, I saw Modran on the ferry, standing before the mail coach joking and laughing with the boatmen and the other passengers. He petted an obsequious dog. If the dog had been a girl, the dog would have slapped his chin with a rose. I thought of the girl and her rose of course and knew that was not the first time a rose had met his chin. He had been on this road before and suddenly I felt as though I had been on it all my life.

"When the ferrymen came over this morning, they said a skinny woman with a purple hand had been found on the eastern shore. I could not believe them. I had looked everywhere for you. Did you not see the torches on the far side of the river?"

"It was foggy."

"Of course it was. That is why I worried so, especially after that ridiculous assumption of yours about that barn girl. And now you expect me to believe you? That you swam across the Elbe at night? Do you think I am a fool? You had me worried to death. Did you take up with some boatmen? Give them a quick fuck with that bloody pussy of yours for passage?"

"Of course not, I went in to bathe and I fell in. The current was strong. I only went in to bathe because of my 'bloody pussy,' you monster. What boatman would fuck me? You have all my possessions, what would I do?"

"And little thanks I have for that. Here is your bag with your things, clothes, your shoes, boots, and that old Hagen fisherman's sweater. Why do you keep that thing? Was it some sailor's you fancied?"

"Yes you ass, it was my father's."

"Why isn't he wearing it?"

"It's not really his, but he wore one just like it."

"Typical of you. You say one thing but really mean another. I don't know why you just can't tell me the truth."

"Tell me again, Modran. How was I supposed to run away with nothing but my shift?"

"Here, you are bleeding again," he said, shoving an old rag toward me. "I think you'll have to ride outside."

"Yes, I should want some fresh air. It's stale in there," I said.

The mail coach climbed away from the Elbe, and I lost sight of it in the haze. I had long lost sight of the mountains. I missed them. The Sun seemed particularly bright as it rose above the mist, and yet the air felt yellow and sickly-warm.

The strange nightdreams of the River, of the lands I had crossed—under there? My head ached with the thought of it, but I remembered the Moon last. He had drawn me into the water and I began to understand the ways of the Water a little better.

"Amor est luna," I said to the driver, who pretended not to hear me. I thought of the Moon, somewhere on the other side of the world. The Moon sailed over darkling waters there, elusive and hidden in clouds, but he would burst out and make promises to a girl in the Japans. She waited for her husband to return from his first wife. The Moon told the girl that she was the husband's favorite. So the Moon lied as well as the Sun. And the truth of the Water was always reflected. I closed my eyes to the Sun above me and tried to imagine the Elbe as the mail coach careened and cathocked its way along the road. I stepped into the River over and over and each river became a new river.

The coach did not loll along like the von Duschter carriage had. We were not royalty but travelers only. I began to wonder if we were thieves. Why were we traveling in a mail coach, of all things? I remember he had said it was the only thing we could have found in Bärenburg that would take us to Spandau at the time, and I believed this. I believe it now.

It led to a deeper question of why we took the southern, slow way. He claimed the Mödeburg Road was too crowded, that the southern road we took was more leisurely. It had been wonderful to have the wide-open world before me, to make love in fields, to share the cherries with him on the road, but were those moments not all parts of his design? As we continued onward to Spandau, the cherries lost their savor in my memories. I thanked the gods that I was bleeding and not bearing his child.

We stopped in a town called Zirwisti for the night. I lay on the floor, for my flow was heaviest at that point and I often had to change the rags between my legs. I did not want to touch Modran, and I knew he felt the same of me.

"Why did you leave Hagen, Ada?"

"I was pregnant with a man's child. A married man."

"That is no reason to leave. Many women like you would have stayed. You could have remained out of sight; perhaps he could have supported you and your child."

"It had to do with the library. I could not stay there."

"I see. You did not want to have his child. And so you didn't, did you?"

"No, I did not."

"That is because you are selfish. I've seen it. This desire to be alone, even when you are in my arms. You have grown cold to me since those bedbugs ate you in Bärenburg. Would it help you to know, even though you are lying there in a black puddle of your own hate, that I still fancy you? I still think your intellect and skills would complement mine upon some endeavor. The bookstore is still not out of the question for me—is it for you?"

What a cruel question. I had promised myself I would not cry in front of him anymore. He didn't deserve it—yet the tears were there in the darkness. My face was away from him. I was thirsty. The pitcher of water I fetched was cool and boiled with some few tea leaves in it, and I choked and gasped it down, blubbering into it.

"Well? Do you not wish to come to Spandau? I can send you back to the mountains now if you'd rather be there, but I don't think they would have you. It sounds as though you have burned your bridges across the Elbe into Hagen as well. If you will allow it, things will be better, as they once were, once we get to Spandau."

"Do you promise?"

"Yes, Ada, will you promise things will be better?"

"Yes. I promise things will be better," I said.

And so I stayed with him. What had I been running away from? Had it not become a new pursuer? Did not each step forward move behind to pursue me? These questions plagued me but none more so than: where would I go? What would I do if he left me by the road? I tried to remember my journey across the river. Or was it under? Through? The great distances, where were they? How did I not drown? But my thoughts returned to the very real dry reality of being alone yet with him.

The next day, we waited in the postal yard and I listened to the driver's fear of the Ravenswald.

"There are a band of thieves said to be there, and a coach is too fat of a target. We shall wait. I understand a troop of the Emperor's cavalry is coming and we can go with them."

Come they did. They were proud men in cuirasses, with lances, guns, and feathers flowing from their wide-brimmed hats. They were handsome men even though their task was gruesome.

Modran noticed as I watched them refresh themselves before going through the forest.

"I was a soldier once, did I tell you that?" Modran said.

"No, but it doesn't surprise me somehow."

"Yes, I was an engineer for the city of Amsterdam. I helped with the defense against the Spaniards. I made a fine sight on the lines, inspecting, pointing out what needed to be done, but it was dreary work. I found ordering men about to be tiring. And the stink! There was no glory in digging undermines and dirty fighting."

"Did you kill anyone?"

"Yes, of course. I had to. Three Spaniards once, from Cadiz I think. They were attempting to destroy one of the main dikes that protected the city. Had to kill them with my bare hands because we did not want to alert their ship, which was just out of sight in the darkness. But we knew she was there. And when I had killed them, we lured her in with a signal until the long guns could sink her."

"You sound proud of this."

"It was an accomplishment, but I feel no great pride in it. Once the siege lifted I left as quickly as I could."

Although we attempted to follow the cavalry, they were too swift upon their horses. They were in no mood for slowing down their pace with an old mail coach, yet the coach driver felt their swath would be a good insurance against thieves and he set the horses to follow in their wake as quickly as he could.

This meant the coach ride was the roughest, jolt-filled stretch of the trip. I was still bleeding and felt sick. It was hot, so I only wore my shift and pressed my legs together as hard as I could while I lay down on the roof of the coach. Modran had said the fresh air outside the coach would do me good, but the bouncing line of the horizon made me vomit twice. I think he was just happy to be rid of me. The coachman did not seem to care.

I remember the Sun not shining on me and the sounds changing as we went deeper into the Ravenswald. The air smelled of fir and the deep green humus of a forest in the busiest of seasons, where each tree grew as quickly as it could, drank as much from the earth as possible, and considered the finery of its leaves.

Yet I was sick from the road, sick of myself, sick of everything, so I was not strong enough to even lift myself to see who it was who had fired the musket shot in front of us.

The coach came to a halt. There was a cacophony of horses shrieking and men yelling.

"B'gods, don't kill me—take whatever you want!" screamed the driver.

"What have you? Get down from there!" A hand reached into my hair and pulled me down off the coach, causing me hit my head against the rear wheel as I tumbled hard to the ground. I was not knocked unconscious, but my memories of what happened next are clouded from poor perspective, blurry vision, fear, and anger.

"She's on the red-rag, this witch."

"Does she have any money?"

"Get your hands off me!" It was Modran's voice.

"You look good, my friend. Step out of there or we will shoot you and your witch."

The Sun was shining on us in a glade. The horses and several men in masks and kerchiefs stood in a circle. My head pounded, and I felt hands all over me tearing my shift. Soon I was left on the ground naked and bloody.

"There's nothing here—she's got nothing on her, not even any meat—and it's bad luck to rape a witch when she's on her red-rag."

"Search the coach—most of it's mail you say?"

The coach driver was more than obliging.

"I think so. Tear it apart. You know your business."

There was another conversation. I remained on the ground but could hear Modran speaking with someone of some eloquence, whom I took for the leader. When I brushed my hair away from my face, covered with leaves and blood, I felt a gash on my head.

"We have nothing. I have spent the last of my funds on this very trip."

"I do not believe you."

"What do you wish, for me to strip naked?"

"Perhaps. Where are the rest of her clothes?"

"In there, she probably has some money sewn away, I'm sure of it," one of the thieves said. They dumped out all of my clothes, tearing them apart. My purse fell to the ground. At this I screamed, but it was dry and hollow.

"You have our thalers, now will you leave us in peace?" Modran asked.

"We should kill you, for you know us now."

"I cannot see your face, although I would guess you are a Doktor from the way you are dressed."

"Perhaps I am, which would make your life even more precarious. Who is this scribner from Hagen? Is she your wife?"

"No, she is my secretary."

"She is tall and looks very miserable now." A long-nailed hand brushed the hair away from my face, for I was lying on my side. The Doktor gently lifted my chin. "I apologize, Ms. Scribner. Usually when we rob someone they are not in such a state of disrepair. For this, I will spare you, and none of the boys seems to want a piece of your tail now anyway. It would seem that bad luck is good luck for you, nonetheless. These thalers of yours will do nicely as compensation. Now now, do not cry. I will leave you these pretty shoes, for I will have no use of them, but the old boots are quite nice. Remember that it is better to live than—well—not. "

I closed my eyes and wished he would have killed me.

Later, I heard Modran's voice: "Come on; help me get her in there."

"We'd best get a blanket for her; she'll get cold before we reach Ravenstein," the coachman said. "I've got a blanket for the horses under the seat, sir. It's old and red. No harm done to it you know. Her head's cut bad, sir."

"Well, what can we do about that? We must get to Ravenstein."

People have always thought I am frail because I am thin. Yet I surprise them when I eat and I surprise them when I'm strong. I never fully lost consciousness in the whole ordeal.

"I am sorry, Ada. I am so sorry," Modran said. He looked down at me. I would not speak. I couldn't at the time, for I was mute from the shock.

"You must understand, if they did not have the money, they would have killed us. And if they thought you really were my wife, I am sure they would have killed you just to pain me."

I supposed he was right, and I thought he was a lying shit. The paradox made me hate him all the more. I was thirsty. Why couldn't he stop talking? But while his words rambled on, all I could think of was water.

After leagues, it seemed, we reached Ravenstein in the dark. We stopped at the postal inn and there, still wrapped in a blanket, I was given water and some broth.

"She'll need proper rest tonight, sir, and she can stay here for that. My husband will see that you're seen to. Goodnight."

The hostler's wife and his daughters took to washing me in a tub they used for butchering pigs, which I now look on as ironic—but then it was the purest form of comfort I could imagine. After the bath, the women put an old shift on me, then gave me a few more rags and gently carried me to a large bed.

"Don't worry about the shift, ma'am. I think you're almost finished anyway. That's what they get for taking that road so fast and with Doktor Kreidler about. No wonder. Poor child. Here, Ada. That is your name, I understand. It will burn a bit going down, but you've had this before, I'll wager, when they did this," she said, pointing to my tattooed hand. "They're quite beautiful, you know" She then gave me a ladle full of fiery Spandauer schnapps, which did burn, but it left my eyes heavier than hammers and I was soon asleep.

Aside from bangs, bruises, and the cut on my head, I was no physically worse for the experience. My spirit was something else, and I wish I could say that I remained there to heal it, but we remained only two days. I did not see very much of Modran and did not want to.

My hostess, Gertrude, was a happy woman, with enormous hips from bearing six children, four of whom had lived past twelve years old. She was correct about my monthly time passing quickly, and I felt strong enough to walk on the second day. The family was most gracious, and I later learned that their eldest daughter was an imperial scribner as well, and they were quite proud of her.

When I felt ready to walk about, Gertrude gave me an old dress of hers.

"I'm sorry, it's not black and, well, it will only go to your calf. It doesn't fit me anymore, but you're young and you might look quite nice in it." It was brown and made of coarse linen and wool. The laces were old leather, and it was far too big for me. She then tied around me a mustard-yellow apron covered in stains of blood from strangling and butchering chickens.

"You must look Dora up if you are going to Spandau, Miss," Gertrude told me.

On the second day, I went out into the hostler's yard and sat down with Modran beneath a chestnut tree.

"I wish I could stay here," he said.

"Do you?"

The thought of him here deflated me, for I had wanted to stay. I had spent my convalescence imagining tending to chickens and cleaning out stables. Perhaps marrying some farm hand, who, if he loved me and was illiterate, would be the perfect hero to rescue me from the idiocy into which I had placed myself.

"Yes, in a way, but it's just a fantasy. I am sure this life here is hard or boring or both. You must understand, I am sorry. I do not have any more money. What little I stashed away in the door of the coach paid for our continued journey. I do not think you remember, but if I hadn't told them about your money, I'm sure you would be dead."

"I remember. The lie about my position as your secretary was the same sort?"

"Yes, you do remember. You must know that is true. I will make this up to you in Spandau, I promise."

"How? You have no money, Modran."

"Not here. My commission is there, Ada, please remember that! I will put us in a nice inn so you may rest properly. I think we should be going as soon as possible to get there."

"I look terrible and do not feel much better."

"You may stay at the inn as long as it pleases you, but when you're ready, you can go to a real bath there and have all of this terrible journey scoured and purged from your skin, and I will buy you new dresses. Think of it: we are really starting over again."

"Yes, we are. Or I am. You still have your clothes."

"Only these. They destroyed the rest of mine, as well. You actually look rather fetching in a farm dress. If that was just cut smaller for you. And I like you barefoot, you know."

I did not smile. I was in no mood for his jests and I could not understand him at all by that point. He appeared to be concerned for me. He appeared to be everything I had remembered in Visingotha. But he was a coward. Why did he not protect me? Why did he leave me up on the roof of the wagon like a side of pork for the flies? Why did I not ask him these questions?

"You will see," he said, "that it's beautiful on the Platz at night, for it is lit with lanterns in the summer and all manner of musicians will come and there is beer and cider and clear cool wine from the deepest cellars. Wiesingthal's will be where we go for a dress. There is a fine hairdresser there I believe—the Graffin Brandauer uses her and we can get you a new haircut—new clothes, a regal treatment for your body. You will be a new woman, Ada, and then we—"

He went on and on and I felt very tired listening to him. I wanted to go to Spandau, to see it, to reenter the world, but I felt groundless. The chestnut tree's five-fingered leaves shook above me in the gentle wind. I remembered the story from France. This is not how it had turned out for the mother of chestnuts, though Modran's serpentine character was somewhat accurate. The leaves did look like thousands of hands, all waving together in some great crowd of import, but if it was applause or warning or jubilation or lamentation, I could not tell. I did not have the ear for it then. I left him talking there on the seat beneath the tree.

"I'm tired, Modran. I'm going to sleep now. Forgive me. I shall be ready to leave tomorrow."

And I returned to the bed Gertrude had made and slept to my word.

Spandau

As ever it seemed on our journey, we made our arrival at dusk. Modran had sheepishly invited me back into the coach, but he kept a respectful, perhaps contrived distance. I looked out the window as we drew closer and saw Spandau illuminate the night; the Moon was new, so that a faint glow was there against the sapphire and later indigo of the sky. We passed miles of houses, huts, halls, plazas, and circles. I noticed that these had all been once villages and had grown together under the vast skirt of the Imperial City. I dozed a bit at the sameness of it all, but suddenly I was jolted wide awake, and my heart skipped in surprise; my body expected another robbery. The coach did not stop.

"What happened?"

"What do you mean?"

"What is wrong with the coach?"

"Nothing, we have reached the Kaiserway."

"Oh, it's pavement!"

For the rest of our ride we laughed, for we realized that it was something I had forgotten about for nearly eight years. Camaraderie, love perhaps, passed over our faces and we somehow ignored the previous few days, as he described the paving beneath the coach. I inched closer to him again and remembered the brickwork pavement of Hagen.

"The Keeper here is a good man and will honor my credit. I am sorry that the arrangements are not as grand as you may have thought, but we are in reduced circumstances. It will be mended soon."

The Küschner Inn was not grand, nor was it small. It was in an out-of-the way part of town and unremarkable in a seeming lack of both wealth and poverty. After talking with Modran for an hour, the landlord gave the key to an attic room.

"We must be careful now, Ada. Please be with me now. There is much to do and while I do not doubt we shall once again be in better places, we cannot afford to trip up."

"How can we? We don't have any money for the liars and cheats to steal."

"I will have my commission soon, tomorrow. Then, we can start anew."

Modran was gone in the morning. He returned late, beaming that tomorrow we would go get me a new dress. The full amount had to transfer in the bank, he said, but we had enough to buy some things. I was hopeful, for once. Although there was a ewer and basin of water in the room, I was still not accustomed to look into the Water, for I was still too afraid of what immediate calamities no doubt awaited me. Had I been bolder, perhaps I would have turned the Water to my advantage, yet ignorant as I remained, and firmly enfranchised in the faith of pessimism, I discovered no reason to confirm my fears. We slept in the bed together, but clothed and apart. I wanted to thank him for his restraint, for I was not sure I could ever love him again.

The next day, we did not go to Fergenstreet and its expensive shops. Modran was waiting for the rest of the commission money to transfer and thought it best we get something practical and worthwhile. I had not stood for a dress since Visingotha, and even then it was for the half-blind old sewing woman in town who worked for the mine and mended the officers' clothing. And yet here I did not care if I was not surrounded yet by silks, for the seamstress we visited had beautiful linens of purples and crimsons: my favorite colors. I stood and she measured me for all, and I got two new shifts as well.

"Since you need a dress now, I have one I made for a banker's notary, miss. It is not a fancy Hagen purple, but all black. However, I think it will fit you because she was tall and thin like yourself. For a few thalers I—"

"Think nothing of it, it is hers." Modran said and he tossed a purse of money onto the table. "I need to get you out of that sack cloth from Ravenstein. Well," he started laughing at his own unintentional ribaldry, "and you may need to wear something between now and when your fancy dress is ready."

The dressmaker was right; the plain scribner's dress fit me perfectly and she said the purple dress would be ready within three days. Modran took me to one of the enormous baths in the center of the city and I was washed clean of the road. We even lounged together, naked in the main bathing hall, and talked of plans. But later, we did not make love.

There was still a distance that I sought to keep and he made no effort to cross it.

Over the next few days Modran would always return late at night, and while his clothes sometimes smelled of smoke, he did not sound nor smell drunk. He would light a candle and sit for a while. I rubbed his feet, for he said they ached from walking so much, and there were all manner of business opportunities one night that were gone the next. A bookseller's shop in Mödeburg had already sold, and then a printer with a license in England had just died and the King seized his assets for the brewing war with France.

"I will be damned if I return to buying cheese though. Enough of that. We should go to the western continents. I know a luthier who moved to New Amsterdam, you know."

He would nod and then sleep soundly into the next day.

I went and retrieved the dress myself on the third day, and it was beautiful. The purple bodice and sleeves fit me tightly, with embroidered swallows darting amongst cunning peacocks, and it went beautifully with Benjamin's shoes. I bought an English bonnet to go with it such as those I had seen the other women wearing.

"My daughter does the needlepoint, Ms. Ludenow. When I told her of your ... hand, if you will excuse me, she grew quite excited. You see there are swallows." I met her daughter, who was a plain, simple girl of fifteen perhaps, but she was crippled below the waist and so did not leave her mother's shop. We talked of travels and her large black eyes grew wider when her mother informed her that thieves had stolen my clothes.

"Stripped them from your body?"

"They cut them apart. They thought I had stitched money into my clothes. It was a mistake."

"I do not think so. It seems smart to me. Perhaps we can offer that for travelers, mother."

"It is an old trick, my dear, and that is why they cut up her clothes."

It felt wonderful to talk to people and to finally walk around the city. I met two scribners of Spandau at a fruit market: a blonde and brunette in black with their hair tied up, for it was warm that day. They were poking at apples with their black fingers, for the scribners of the Emperor only have their thumbs and first two fingers tattooed, unlike the entire hand, as in Hagen. Although they worked in the library, they knew of the hostler's daughter, and gave me directions to the Emperor's mail hall, which was the main postal and communication nexus of the city, as well as where the scribners' dispatch hall was.

"It's next to the Hallward's Hanseatic Hall. You can't miss it," the blonde said. "It's just like us, you know, for it's a thin, graceful building behind the fat Hallward's palace. And it's closest to the stables!"

The better part of a fortnight had gone by and Modran still had said nothing about any impending situation. I awoke one morning and he was there, having come in very late again. What was I to do? I felt that we had fallen into a sort of routine, but the fire of our romance remained utterly extinguished on the banks of the Elbe. Was that what my journey through the Water had told me? I lay awake listening to him breathe and thought about that journey. The Water, I realized, never showed me things as they are. There were seldom any clear visions, and much of the geography was either distant or fantastic. I assumed this was how it worked. That I was unclear myself—and that this helped cast the Water's visions into vague metaphors—did not occur to me.

I had thought of leaving him—pursuing another commission and going Elsewhere. I was not sure he cared, and this gnawed at me. He had been pleasant, even affectionate at times. He pressed himself against me and I could feel his arousal, but I could not love him, yet part of me wished to return to the far bank across the river. I felt my own desire rise again, but why for him? We were doing nothing, and this too disturbed me. I thought surely something would come about that would improve our situation, and then I could decide if the torn love could be mended. While I still had not entirely forgiven him for everything, I felt better having regular meals and real clothes again, and those were perhaps the start of my new life with him. As the morning wore on, I thought of Elsewhere again. Did I really wish to go there?

I gently shook him and he reached out to me. He caressed my arm, then my breast, and I let him for a moment.

"No, not yet."

"When?"

"You must understand my concern: my shyness. So much happened on the road. So much seems to have changed here. I appreciate your generosity, but I worry—"

"We are fine on money now, if that is what you are worried about. You see your fine dress gains you access where otherwise you would be suspect. You look very astute and powerful now. But since you do not wish to make love, I need to sleep. The salt merchant I am to see tonight likes his cups, and I need my rest."

"Does he not conduct business in his hall? I have not seen you much at all these days."

"No, they do not do things like that here, at least the preliminaries. It is drinking and cards, if you must know, and since my old military days I can manage the pretense of indulging heavily without actually losing my wits or money."

"Oh, I was hoping to go out together. It's a fine day."

"Ada, I brought you on this journey so that you could enjoy this city the way you were meant to. Remember our conversations on the hill?"

"I just would perhaps want some company. To start again."

"You told me you have new acquaintances at the library. Go to the Eugen Gardens when they are done and have a fine roast chicken and some Kölsch and think of me."

"I would, but I think you wish to be rid of me."

He then sat up in bed and looked at me. He was still handsome—still a rugged, elegant man. I felt myself wanting him again, but his mood shifted and I knew him well enough to be frightened.

"Why is it, Ada, that every conversation we engage in is like Rome, in that all roads lead to Ada, and Ada alone? It's like you are this great city and must know how you are being served, and so you stretch out your nets this way and that to capture some remark about yourself, and like an octopus you will dart out long enough to capture a ship if none come by."

I snickered then. "That does not even make any sense, are you confusing spiders with octopuses?"

And then he slapped me across my face. It was not a fist, but it was a first. "Damn you, you cold bitch. How dare you laugh at me, like some commoner? Well you are, aren't you? Deep down you're always like the rest of them. Both of them have eight legs. I cannot help it if you are so literal that you follow and limp along behind my thoughts. Take yourself to your sacred fucking library. I have work to do here. Important work in this city. I have my commission for the delivery, but I must make that into something else. Now leave, I'm going to sleep. I'm sorry I struck you but I'm very tired. Be here tonight when I return, for I shall need you to write down our accounts before I go to meet the salt-merchant, if you are so interested in my company."

The porter noticed the imprint of his hand on my face as I left. I followed the streets I knew until I reached the library. The scribners I had met were not there that day. I tried to read, but all I could manage was a great deal of glowering. I bit at my hair. I picked and bit at my nails. Finally, when I returned to the inn, Modran was not there and I was glad.

I looked in a basin of water and spoke his name once. The Water clouded as it always did, then drew clear and black as though it was reflecting the night sky, even in the daylight. So the sight was still with me and there was Modran.

He was sitting before a grand carven portal to a cave. That it was a rich dwarves' cave riddled with gold I had no doubt, even though I could not peer into it. He had a rich hat I hadn't seen before with a red feather of some incredible bird. A beautiful woman who looked like me walked out and took his hand. He kissed her hand graciously, and I noticed that my hair was not right. It coiled and moved in the wind of the water and became flame. I led him into the cave and I could see the gold glittering in the fires of that place. Griffins and rich men danced beyond, though I could not see them clearly. And so there he was, seeking for our fortune. Or perhaps his.

More days passed and I spent most of them in the library where I found refuge in information and news from all over the world. While the stacks of books, scrolls, and papers were cordoned off from most of the visitors, I could read in the reading room. The air in the reading room was hazy, on account of the smoking. I felt irritable and sick and so moved off into the private sections, where I found a nice booth and read on hydromancy.

I missed Benjamin very much then, for he was such a kind and patient man. I wondered and daydreamed—my first foray into truly subjunctive nostalgia—for what if I had seduced him? It would not have been hard, I realized. Perhaps we could have run away together. He was not handsome. He was shorter than I was, but he was smart and faithful. I thought we could have loved one another far more than the two people we engaged. I then realized that his fidelity is what made him attractive. I did not really wish to steal him from his simple but pleasant wife, but that he could have made such a troth made him a King among lesser men whose bloodlines of nobility were an accident of fate.

Of how I came to possess the Watersight, the books had numerous explanations, many of which seemed ludicrous and easy to discount. I had not made love with a narwhal beneath the northern lights during the winter solstice. I had not been stirring the cauldron of a Welsh wisewoman at any time in the recent past, nor had I rubbed the ointment meant for a dragonet or elfling on my eye after assisting in such midwifery. Fruchwalter was the closest, and I remembered

Benjamin again. He had offered me this very book. How stupid I was.

Bathing in the pool of the Rubezahl is the most efficacious way to see the world of those who live on the other side of Water and much that happens in this world as well. He will often transform himself into a pool, or enter into one if he thinks a comely woman will bathe in it, for in this way he enjoys and enters her body. She will often have the Watersight afterward, especially if she drinks of the water while bathing and does pleasure herself there as well which is nigh impossible to resist since his caresses and whispers of lust are most pleasing to women's ears or those men who do hear them, for it was said that Ravenuüoloki did become a mare ...

Fruchwalter was a terrible writer and the rest of the entire section, which was one long sentence, strayed off into Norwegian religion.

Schinderdottir had some description of method:

The Pool does not always show what is. Because we look so much at the world, it is the sense we notice first, reflected in the Pool, yet it changes things. For the Pool to work most excellently, it is necessary to immerse oneself, but one must be very careful. At this point the Hydromancer is not merely observing the world of the Water-people from afar but has entered into it.

It is good to bring a talisman with one while entering the Water. Only the strongest magicians and doctors should enter the Pool naked unless they bring with their souls some bond that lashes them firmly to this world. It is said that menstruating women have the strongest power.

The Waterpeople are exceedingly beautiful. In the Rus they have entire kingdoms below the waves, and I am led to believe that many of the Faery kingdoms in the old Celtic Lands are linked to this empire by means as yet undiscovered.

The book, which stood on the bank of interest to me because it was closely describing my experiences of looking into the Water, then became another catalog of Kingdoms. I was unsure of why scholars were so keen on indexes and lists when they never explained how one should experience any one component. But then does anyone stop and study one brick on the road, even though it's a marvel in itself? But the item about menses snapped me awake. I counted on my hands and realized that the Watersight had been strongest just before and during my time. How else to explain that strange journey under the Elbe?

It had been well over three weeks since my last time, and I had not had sex with Modran since the Elbe. What would I see now? I had just seen him again in the Water—in a wash basin of all things—and I feared what may be coming. So I went and bought some hashish tobacco to take my mind off of it and read Panderfloss's poetry.

Freedom and happiness are not the same predicate. This simple line, pedantic though it was, made the most sense to me of everything I had read that day.

A few more days went on in this manner. Modran would often return late, when I was already sleeping. He slept in late and I woke up early, as always, with the Sun. There was always a purse of money by the bed, and Modran bade me to take as much as I needed while I tried to silently leave.

"Go to the bath, have a scrub" he might say. "Go to Fergenstreet and pick out your fabric. We will go the day after tomorrow."

And yet we never did. I did chat with the two librarians, but they were hard at work and we never could find the time to visit the Eugen Gardens.

One day, my head and neck ached me terribly, so I left the library and returned early, for I wanted to lie down at the inn. Two of the inn's chambergirls were scrubbing the floor. One of the chamber girls was proud and assured. She was a thick, big chested thing, with blonde plaits in her hair, and the other was mousy. They had not heard me, for it was an early afternoon.

"This morning?"

"It's wonderful. He waits until the skinny one leaves. I don't know where she goes. I'm not even sure he fucks her."

"Like he does you?"

"I'm not a skinny witch, I may not be much but I know what a man likes."

"A man likes much, maybe he likes to talk to her. And then there's the Graffin he is seeing, I've heard."

"He's got a nice a big thing and a honeyed tongue. He's come here before, you know. Gets his money off the Graffin of Brandauer. He's over there now, with his tongue in her somewhere, I'm sure."

"No one knows where he is from," said the mousy one. "He told me he was from Hagen."

"He told me he was from Italy. It doesn't matter. He'll go away again. Bit of fun. Like the summer fair."

I knew the Graffin of Brandauer would be in the catalogue. It was all so clear now: I was not sure how vast the catalogue was, but I was sure that I was one small book among a great many other volumes. I stood in the doorway, shaking with rage and the confirmation of everything I had feared. The girls stopped their stupid laughter when they saw me. I wanted to kill the slattern, but she just looked down and sneered.

And there in the bucket's dirty water, murked with shoe muds and oils, I saw him. I knew his back, his naked arms. I could feel their ghosts upon my own. I watched him join with a red-headed woman upon a bed: he had buried himself up to his balls in her. Her face gleamed white beneath her powder, her lips were red like a bloody cherry in a field of snow, and her mouth groaned open. It was a moist, howling sort of hole, because Modran's cock was deep in her. I knew what he was capable of.

This vision was in the still time of the present. In time, he leaned away from her, leaned back upon the bed. He held her head, forcing her down on his member, and asked her while he fucked her mouth: "Whom do you love more, yourself or me?"

And then I came to the problem, because when he stroked her hair back, expecting her answer, the other woman he was face-fucking became me. I was mute. What else could I say with his cock in my mouth? I looked and saw another woman, another me sitting clothed in a chair, watching the lovers.

I stood looking at the Water and was furious. I dug my nails so far into my hands that I bled by my palms like the Christians who so crave the passion of their God that they share his wounds of the cross.

"Don't you love me?" he asked. "Without me you would not even be here." I moaned an answer as best I could and his hips entered that fractured rhythm men perform when they are about to come. He shouted to the world and no one in particular, save perhaps himself, for he was the world.

But then I saw the red-headed woman again, swallowing

his semen. The woman in the chair was her now, dressed in finery, her bosom tightly strapped, and her hair up in a style that equaled my annual wages at least. She looked at me and asked:

"How else shall you know the world until you give yourself up, as we have done?"

I angrily kicked the bucket over and the slattern awkwardly crouch-crawled backwards, tangling in her skirt. She yelled some profanity at me, but I straightened my clothes and left. I was nearly out the front door when the landlord at the counter cleared his throat.

I stopped and turned my head to him.

"Yes?"

"Ms. Ludenow, with regard to the matter of your bill."

"Yes?"

"It has been some days now since Mr. Modral has paid anything save the deposit. As his secretary, I hoped you may be able to take care of this matter. I did not wish to bother him with the details."

I clenched my fists, my ass, my calves, my teeth, and, I think, even my ears.

"Ah," I said, composing myself as much as possible and walking over to the counter. Although it was on a riser, I still met the landlord's eyes. "Mr. Modral has not informed me of this. I apologize."

"Well, if you would be so kind. I have the sum here."

I remember that he spun the ledger on the counter and shoved it at me. The sum was actually not as much as I feared because Modran was cheap after all, but it was enough to make me feel trapped, to make my throat feel dry and closed.

"I am going to see him just now and will inform him. You

must understand I cannot sign over any sum until I clear it with him and retrieve it from the Temple Bank first. Do not worry, it is only a matter of procedure."

"Of course, when?"

"When we return, I hope. Now, if you desire the money tonight, I shall need to leave immediately to inform my master and make the draw from the bank."

"Of course, thank you Ms. Ludenow. Thank you."

I was dressed in my purple dress and I wore my hair tucked under my English bonnet. I looked like any other professional scribner. But beneath my skirt, my legs were particularly angry that day. Every inch of me, from toenails to fingernails, was angry. Every hair on my head, my pits, and my below stood on end, it seemed. This wrath gave my stride an extra length and speed with each step.

People were helpful.

"Oh, the Von Brandauer House is at the end of Fergenstreet, just before it gets to the Imperial Circle."

I found Fergenstreet without difficulty and walked by the atelier Wiesenthal's & Co. This was the establishment I had seen in the brook on the wide Elbe Plain. I went around to the servants' entry and asked for Mr. Modral or the Graffin. An assistant seamstress told me they had not been in for a week, but that the Graffin's dress was ready for a final fitting. I gladly volunteered to take a note for her and, armed with this ticket, I walked to the grand house.

Such wealth had become known to me during my stay, but only in façades, the manner of wealth that faces the outside world. The masons had made the fluted and intricate joinery stonework resembling imps and walkuras, daemons and flying men. They looked down on me in amusement, crowded above lintels, attics, and long windows. I scuttled beneath them around to the monolithic, flat, and ugly side of the building where the servants let me in and allowed me to sit in the kitchen. The assistant hallward took the note regarding the dress and said she would find Master Modral, for he was in conference with the Graffin.

The kitchen was vast, made to serve many mouths. A fire burned in the hearth and two cooks looked at me with indifference. One of them was a young man of sixteen, perhaps. His skin was clear and perfect. He possessed a pouting, heart-shaped mouth and deep blue eyes. These were framed by wide cheekbones and a fringe of light brown hair. He looked Wendish or perhaps Russian, and he was beautiful. He finally smiled at me. His teeth were rotted, and he knew this, so he closed his lips bashfully, but I smiled back.

The old cook, a thick, thumb-shaped woman with a barrel gut, thin hips, and no breasts ignored me and peeled potatoes. I approached the youth and looked down at him. I ran my finger along his arm.

"Yes, Madame Scribner?" he asked.

"Has he made love to you as well? Please tell me. He said he does not mind your teeth when he is inside of you, doesn't he? He says that you are beautiful."

The old woman snorted and looked at me in anger, but I stared down at her in my wrath. I looked again upon at the young man; his blush told me everything. But then Modran rushed in.

"What are you doing here!?" Modran whispered this as loudly as he could.

He sounded like a snake and so I told him so: "Master, your forked tongue is wiggling. Do not be cross; I have merely come here to inform you of the lodging bill that you have allowed into arrears and to also give the hallward here a note from Wiesenthal's & Company that Her Grace's dress is ready for final fitting."

"You bitch, turn around and get out of here right now." He grabbed my wrist and marched me out of the kitchen like a child. He pushed me out into the daylight toward a two-horse trap.

We rode back angrily, awkwardly, silently, for the trap was open. I guessed that he was perhaps fucking the hallward as well, who arranged this convenience for him. We stopped early.

"The entrance is that way."

"Be quiet, you know we cannot go in that way. Come with me." We got off the horse-trap and went in through the servants' entrance. He kicked open the door and the mousy chamber girl, who was stirring a pot of stew, jumped. Modran put one finger to his lips and we passed by her and went up the back stairs.

Once the door shut he started: "How dare you!"

"How many lies is it Modran? Is this another one? I am not sure. I'm so stupid, I doubt I can count high enough."

He slapped me then and I fell on the bed.

"I am trying to set us up in a situation where we can leave this place, do you not understand that? You have to wine and dine the money out of these people."

"Meaning that you are a confidence man and I am your secretary."

"In a word, yes. You can take it or leave it right now, Ada, but you have nothing without me and you know that."

"And you cheated von Duschter out of his carriage."

"Yes."

"That was why Jorgi was so agitated and you wanted to get out of the mountains and off the plain so quickly."

"Yes."

"And so we never had enough money for a proper carriage when we left Bärenburg."

"Yes."

"And so we really didn't have any money when the thieves robbed us, not because you spent it, but because it wasn't there and talking your way out of things is your greatest gift."

"Yes."

"And you probably never fought in Amsterdam, either, correct?"

"Yes."

"And you did fuck that girl in the barn."

"Yes."

"Yes, yes, yes. Fuck your yeses. Why did you not tell me the truth, or were all those times you loved my body in the mountains for nothing? You knew I was poor. You must have smelled my poverty."

"That is true, Ada." He sighed and sat down on the bed. "Stop in your wrath and think about it. It is true I am drawn to the pleasures of people, but we always spoke the truth of our hearts when we made love. The other people are nothing. What would I be doing with you if I did not love you?"

I could not answer him.

"You are not the most beautiful woman to other men, but you are beautiful to me. It is true, I wanted to understand some of the affairs and accounts of the mine, but I quickly knew that you possessed no great secrets. You only knew the day-to-day items there. And yet you were different. You were passionate and so beautiful in your solitude. I thought if you came with me and shared my life that you would understand."

"Why did you not tell me this?"

"How could I? It is such a thing that once you are in deep, there is only discovery, not revelation. You will want to leave I am sure, but where will you go?"

I did not answer him. I sat on the bed next to him trying to think, trying to understand what he was and what it would mean to be alone. He put his hand on my thigh and then moved it between my legs. I turned and slapped him, but he did not stop. I hit him again. It felt wonderful. He did nothing to stop me, so I hit him yet again. He was very good, because he had worked me up into such a fury that there was only one last thing to do.

We removed our clothes like puppets and fucked like puppets: both of us without passion. I wanted to prove that I was the best for him and I rue not what I did but that I wanted to do it.

I do not know what he wanted, he climbed behind me and I was glad, for it felt the better of our ways to me, and I knew it excited him, so the duration of the act would be short. It was easy to squirm away from him when I felt his rhythm begin that obvious stumble towards his orgasm. I held him down there and finished him with my purple hand. His seed was pearlescent and bright against the tattoos. We stared into each other's eyes. I do not know what I saw there, for his visage and eyes were blank of meaning, like a page that is empty and thrown away in the wet outside. For myself, I was a dry well. There was nothing. I did not reach my own climax and did not wish to.

"You are still important to me, Ada. You are still the one

who knows me best. You know this, I need you. This is not unpleasant to you, I can tell."

I rose from the bed. His seed was now cooled on my breasts, my hand and the tangle of my hair. I sat in a chair. The air was so close—so warm and humid—that I felt it was a new sort of lingering death. Like a lung thick with snot, I could draw no breath of value there. The wood was hard upon my bare skin, my bony ass, my legs, my feet against the rough floor. From that wood I tried to draw strength. I looked at him.

"Do not look at me that way."

"I have looked at you enough, Modran. I saw into the Water and I knew you were not true. How can I tell you this? How will you understand? Should I say the old things and the old courses of words when we first talked on the doorstep of the old mine? Very well. I am naked now, and torn away from the stone like ore, crushed beneath cruel hammers. I am blistered and scarred from the amalgamating baths. I see the stars grow and join into a single sheet of invasive quicksilver. You are nowhere."

"I would have given you everything, Ada. You were different."

"Tell me one thing, for it is what I most want to understand. In all those sunny days on the mountain, in my bed or on the grass beneath the apple trees or in the carriage: how could you lie like that to me? There was no commission. There never was."

"It was easy," he said. "For you already heard me say it in the wishes in your heart and though you discount everything I say and am as lies, know too that sometimes I wish to believe it myself."

I hated that it was summer and I felt more at ease without

my clothing. I very much wanted to be buried alone beneath a pile of furs and woolens in some felt tent far beyond the Urals. I still did not know what to do and I did not want to be alone. So I went back to the bed and lay down. He did not touch me and I did not touch him. I listened to our breaths for hours it seemed, but then at some point I fell asleep, for I awoke quite alone and naked in the darkness.

He left. His few things were gone. There was no note. I curled up on the bed with my arms around my legs, knowing that, with a lie that covered another lie, he had won the game.

The Noon of Love

Anton's shape has changed again. He grows her white skin, so smooth upon his body, and her hair of flame erupts from his head like a goddess. It flickers, moves, and searches, yet it is cold when the tresses wrap around my wrist and waist. His nudity in her beauty is taunting and perfect. Yet he now has my face, my eyes, my long nose, my wide mouth.

"When I asked you to change, the Red Woman's shape was not the one I had in mind."

"Oh but she was very much in your mind. I am trying to understand you, Ada, and this Graffin is you, is she not? What you always wished you were? Did you believe this love for a raconteur, a thief, a mountebank would transform you so?"

So perfect is his form, her form, in detail and shock, that my memory retreats, huddles. It is beaten, and my mind wavers. The stars are wheeling above, and I know I must answer.

"The constancy of his presence lulled me into a hollow comfort that passed the time and allowed me to forget how alone I was in the world. But know that I often asked myself: 'How could I have been so blind?' Perhaps by traveling under the Water, I never gave the ferryman the coins that had covered my eyes."

"You did not wish to face the truth."

"In the vast repository of your being, Anton, you must know that the most efficacious forms of magic are the ordinary ones of desire. They require no powers but skill, and Modran was very skilled at saying what I wanted to hear."

"You believed him, then, about sparing your life when the thieves waylaid you?"

"I had no proof otherwise, and it seemed reasonable. The alternative was too horrible to think. I did not want the light to break me open and turn all the truths into stone toads." I let slip this old hint, the violence of soft pink turning to hard gray, to granites under the eventual rain. He does not seem to notice, to catch, or does he?

"But what is the truth? How could I have known its face and shape at the time?"

"Upon that bed, you loved him."

"I hated him then. I was no longer afraid to."

And yet if you hated him so then why did you copulate with him again? You were afraid he would abandon you. Fear is not hatred, Ada."

"Anton, I have explained this before and evidently not enough. For some of us, making love, or even hatred in this case, is the most intimate thing we can do with each other. In that storm we sink, we unbecome ourselves."

"You mean you die?"

"In a way. That is why some of us call it the Small Death."

"Yes, I have observed it, that oblivion you enter. It is delicious and one of the greatest gifts your evanescent race possesses. It sounds metaphorical. But I am growing used to this talk. I could easily say that I make love with the waterfall when I stand beneath it. I am refreshed and clean. The waterfall has had a small break, a deviation from its normal course, and perhaps it enjoys that. But we part without hurting one another."

"That is a beautiful metaphor."

"I must be catching it, like those diseases you pass from one to another. Tell me, did you really think you became one with this man? I think you wished to overpower him, eat him as I will eat you when this tale is done. You did not wish to understand him. You only wanted to know why you believed his exquisite lies."

"Anton, you cannot know love."

"I have eaten enough of it."

I must show courage. I will risk a little sunlight.

"You cannot know love, for you cannot see the noon. Love hangs in that time of day that would destroy you. Since you cannot experience it, shall I tell you of the Noon of Love? Ah, what is that? From such crimson tresses I see your oak ears grow and unfurl. They cup in curiosity. Very well, let them listen closely."

"On that morning, I reached out for something, and he was not there, so I learned of the Hanging Cold of Noon. Noon came early that morning. The room was warm even though the window was open. The morning air considered its breaths and the motes slowly danced toward the window. Did they know where they are going? Was the sill and beyond a certainty? Perhaps they did not wish to consider the outside.

"Noon said I was a fool to think of the dawn as the red cloaked bird of paradise. I reached out my hand, offering its warmth to the Nothing that gnaws at all of us.

"I remember that his warmth was gone from the pillow and my mind ached to follow his footsteps into the city. I called upon the memories of blossoms, in that they could become almonds, plums, apricots, and cherries. Yet I remembered that all the fruits of the Sun enrobed poisonous stones. That morning, I knew I was alone in my own making and so hung myself at Noon.

"Skinny, my face a joke: perhaps my laugh unsettled him? Perhaps I smelled of piss and disgusted him? I was always too tall, too strange. I was no swan, but only an ugly goose with a long neck. One time, he had said otherwise and kissed me, but a hung bird cannot fly. At Noon on the Day of Love, I no longer believed him. I was always overlooked, left alone. I wore this sentence upon my flat chest and kicked my legs. The rope tightened.

"How much I wished that I was false in my belief on that morning: that Love was a lie. How vast was the tree I hung myself upon. Its branches were many, for I had many doubts that I confirmed and offered to the warm summer morning. Each proof of the falsehood in him was as certain as the breeze, and my unbeliefs grew from limb to branch to bough to twig to leaf.

"I then argued against myself, wrapped in the barrister's black robes of sweet reason: 'Where are all of the old lessons you learned about induction and all of its dragon-headed brood? He was but one lover. If you allow it, your heart will flow with blood and so nourish the cut stumps until two or more toothed heads erupt from your flesh, to feed upon your flesh until you are nothing but mouths and teeth.' "

"Yet reason was a lawyer who argued fruitlessly before a judge who had already made up her mind. Every night would be a prosecution against my heresy in the nihilism of love, ending with an unsleep of sentencing. Every morning Reason would remain by my side as we faced yet another gibbet. Each morning, there was always a last breakfast before I faced the execution of a lonely, barren, childless life.

"I thought of a drunk, hung at noon. He tiptoe-stumbles over the ground, for the noose is tight around his neck and dangles him. The thick rope of wine is the only certainty he knows in the world and so it pulls him on like a toy, hoisting him unto that last Certainty.

"Know that I did love him, Anton. The drunkenness was immediate and complete. I do not know if he ever loved me or if I was just a cunt for his pleasure and perhaps a fond memory. My doubts hung this thought before me that morning and I refused to even take pride in that small accomplishment. Even now I doubt whether he even really hated me, much less loved me."

"But you had doubts upon the mountain—upon the road—and you did nothing," Anton says. "Surely you must feel stupid now."

"Of course, for when I stir the pool of recollection and see the reflections of those old doubts, are they not genuine when time proves them so? Shortly thereafter, I took perverse and bitter pleasure in being right. But that was a long time ago, and I do not feel stupid. Certainly not now. I would have to repeat all of those blunders for that to happen. And I could not do that at the time because I did not know any better. It is an important distinction, you know."

"Why do you speak of Noon as it Was, rather than in the immediacy of Is, as with the other Times of Day?"

There is a brief memory of those times at the beginning, on the mountain. I have examined them many times before I found myself speaking with this troll, and my first feeling is one of hope. It is not even a memory. It is as clear as the feeling of the Water. It is as bright as the nightingale's song; it tastes of certainty, like granite on the tongue. I answer him:

"When Modran and I made love, I spoke myself into timeless oblivion. It is why I shouted so when he entered me. I wanted him to descend upon my flesh and scourge me until there was nothing but the blood and bits of me upon the sheets and the beaten earth of the cabin. When I slept beside him, or thought about him, the immanency of his body and voice defied the count of hours. Do I love him? Did I love him? These questions of tense are bothersome. The freedom of old desire returns in such memories as you have heard earlier in this tale. Those are shorn of those last days in Spandau when I hated him and wished him dead. As I have said, Passion holds the coin of love and hatred on both sides; it spins in the air of recollection, never falling into my hand. I was abandoned in the world again.

"Again?"

"And I am abandoned again when I tell you all of this story. Abandonment requires the constant flow of the past to give it shape and form. But it took me many years to learn that a cartographer of the heart must first possess the expanse of time before she may map it. By mapping it, she may better know how the land was broken."

Lurking

I looked around the bare, plain room one last time. No wonder we were so far out of the way. I was going to be his secretary, after all, and so that was not a lie on the road. Skillful liars always season their work with just enough truth to get by, I realized. But now I had to do something.

I had to sneak out of the inn somehow. I put on Gertrude's old dress and hid my hair under a scarf and attempted to fold and style like the servants of the successful merchant women I had seen in the city. Being unaccustomed to such things, however, I made a shambles of it. I clumsily stuffed my rucksack with only my sweater, writing materials, both the black and purple dresses, my old Harsager book, and my shoes. I threw a sheet from the bed over the bag, bent over, and tried to look like a washer woman.

It is remarkable how absences can remain in our souls. I can still remember the hallway's quiet that morning. The Sun had not climbed very high and so there was no movement in any of the shadowy hallways. I stole down the back stairs on bare feet. I gulped my air as quietly as I could and cursed myself when my bundle would strike the wall or the pilaster as I turned on flights. I cursed Modran for getting a room so high up. I thought maybe he wanted to hide me, or keep me from escaping.

I was nearing one of the last landings when the slattern grabbed my shoulder.

"You're sneaking out of here!" she yelled.

"*Shhh*, I beg you."

"I shall not shush, you bitch, you thieving cunt—I will go and wake the master now,"

"Please don't."

"Get out of my way or I'll break you, you skinny gash!"

Something happened. I still sicken to think of it because it

changed me so utterly, but I forgot myself and forgot Modran, and all I wished to do was kill the girl. I did not see a human girl, understandably stupid. I saw something like a cow—a bag of meat—and I struck her as hard as I could in the face. I struck her as many times as I could as we spun.

My bundle had already dropped with a crash down the stairs, but not as loudly as she did. I followed her and the bundle down, beating on her when she came to a stop.

"What on earth is going on down there?" said a cowardly voice somewhere up above. "Be off with you! I'm coming down with a gun, I swear!" It was the master's voice. I imagined him in his bare legs and nightshirt, a few hairs astray. The quaver in his voice bespoke of thieves and not two ridiculous women fighting.

The slattern was lying on the ground. Her nose was bloody and her elbow was bent in an ugly, unnatural way, but her eyes were open and she was breathing in groans. I leapt over her and raced down the stairs with the last of my things, running out into the street as fast as I could, thankful to be lost in the labyrinth of Spandau.

It was some time until I felt safe enough to stop. My mind raced through the possibilities. The City Guards would be coming for me. They would rape me in the jail, I was sure, and then I would be put on a wheel or torn apart by the horses after they flogged me.

At least there were no bears.

I drank from the Heerische Fountain and knew where in Spandau I was. I relaxed, and smoothed out my clothes, and again tried to look like any other servant woman. I could not wear the purple dress, for that would certainly give me away. So I tied my hair up again as tight as I could. Around me were other women moving with baskets, all of them in white scarfs, mustard-yellow aprons and brown dresses. I said a silent prayer for Gertrude and collected myself not far from the fountain.

I first made an inventory. I still had my seal, of all things, and so I knew I could make some sort of income. I knew I had to leave, but I did not know where to go. "Elsewhere" was perhaps poetically accurate, but not geographically so. I looked through the rest of my rucksack for papers, names of people I knew. Gertrude's daughter was named Dora, but I had no idea if she would be at the Imperial Scribner dispatch or not, for I had never checked. I remembered that Hagen Scribners would be accepted, with lowered commissions, into Imperial Service. It was the only thing I could do. Where would they send me? To Visingotha? I did not wish to slink back there. I was looking for any other clue in my bag when a note fell out of my Harsager book. I did not recognize the paper, nor its Greek imprint. I opened it and struggled through it, for both the writer and I were rusty in our use of that language.

This is close to what I remember it telling me:

Dear Sister,

I am taking two chances in hiding this in your things: that it will be discovered by someone other than you, or that you will not discover it in time. The first I can only address by writing this in Greek, which I believe you will understand. In the second, know that my good wishes go out to you and that you may take some comfort from an old woman.

Modran is a liar and a cheat. He seduced my son. No doubt you have heard some fiction of this story. He seduced me as well—you have probably not heard before. He lies with every breath. He lied to my son and he lied to me and left us with broken dreams and estranged from one another, which is the cruelest blow. As proof of this, ask him of the fantasia "Desire, Do Not Forget Me." His vanity will overpower him and he will claim that he wrote it for my son to perform. My son wrote it for him.

Leave him as soon as you get the chance. My husband is enchanted by him somehow and thinks Modran is a dear friend. You will find many people like this. Avoid them.

Please leave him now and be careful. You bear a Tyrian hand, Sister. You wield great magic with that hand. Go unto the Emperor's Scribners for a commission. You may not get what you want, but I doubt very much you know what that is.

I crumpled the note, not from anger, but in that my hands collapsed together. I cried in the square and people began to look at me. I looked away, my eyes red as roses, and moved off to the shade, to be out of the gaze of the damned Sun. I remained under the stable roof for an hour, perhaps more. I did not count the time, but somehow as the shadows of the buildings deepened and took me in, I realized that I was alive. While the letter was ironically late in discovery, telling me nearly everything I already knew, the fact I was reading it gave me an ontological courage I did not expect.

Later, I stood in the Scrivener's Office and the dispatcher looked at my hand.

"You are wearing a peasant's dress, but that purple, you are a scribner from Hagen? What drives you from that city?" I did not like his tone, not from the aggression, but what he seemed to guess. I decided that perhaps the truth, mixed with the truth I had wished for, was the best answer. I had learned something from Modran

"I was married and my husband abandoned me. I am alone here and I need money."

"You need a commission, in other words. Well, you know that a Hagen stamp is as good as the Emperor's. Why do you need a commission?"

"I have no other situation and wish to leave."

"Yes, well we shall see. You will have to wait until tomorrow or the next day. The hall here is full. I suppose you can share a bed with someone if they'll have you."

I knew by his tone that they, whoever they were, would rather not, and I would also rather not: an arrangement that suited me fine.

"You can find somewhere to sleep, I am sure. It is summer; the nights are warm so you won't freeze near the stables or mail yard. There is a post in the Harz Mountains I have just heard of, for a mining concern. They say the scribner's lover killed the local lord and ran off with his money." He looked at me closely, but not at my face. I looked away and found myself gazing into his tin of water.

I asked the Water for an answer and saw the thick block of desperation that men live in. He wore a bearskin, a hide that would be musty, animal-smelling, and it would be thrown over the bed of moss in his hut. And I saw faces in the water: his wife, perhaps. There was a daughter, for the cast of her face resembled his. I looked back at him and knew what I must do, and knew it would be easier. Everything would be easier.

Friedrich was his name. I learned that afterward. He was married and a few years older than I was, but he was not unhandsome. He bathed, at least, and smelled of water, of man, of tallow soap. It was over quickly; we did not remove our clothes. We lay together in a storage room upon a pile of old mail bags, and I felt like an old mailbag as his semen ran down my leg. He was shorter than I was, of course. I looked down on him afterward; his head was on my breast.

"I am not expecting any payment. I am not a—"

"Let us not talk about it. You think too much, I can tell. I know, because I do it myself. We have a few moments here. Let me pretend that you are the woman I married a long time ago and I can be whatever you wish me to be for a moment or two. For this exchange, you shall have a commission. But you will have it tomorrow before you board the mail coach to Jena."

I sat on hard boards in the common rooms and held my head between my arms. I remember how cool the tender skin just inside my forearms felt. The close memory of lying under the dispatcher did not revolt me when I studied my thoughts, yet the sadness and pathetic nature of the whole affair made me feel small and filthy.

My dignity had retreated to the far side of the world in the previous days and seemed to have remained there. The thought of Von Duschter went through my mind then. I wondered how Modran had killed him. For all of his lies, I had never felt danger, but this revelation chilled me and made my bones feel empty.

It was then I embarked on a long wander through the city, for I was hungry and there was no food at the dispatch hall. I learned many important lessons that day. I learned how to sleep with a man as an exchange. And I learned to sneak out of an inn, although I still had much to learn about fighting.

Two men laughed at me when I walked across Freistreet. I was too ugly and ridiculous to be confused with whores.

Although scribners were well-known in the city, my purple hand drew attention: the Guards would be looking for a Hagen scribner, so I hid my hand in the large folds of Gertrude's dress. I saw the rich merchants, bankers, and nobility ascend and descend from carriages then walk up the front steps of halls, and I grew bitter and furious. Modran was no doubt lying in the arms of such a woman, I thought. My bitterness needed the heat of my mind to make it a bit sharper.

The thought of food drove me to the market. I remembered seeing refuse thrown out that had been perfectly good, while I had absolutely nothing. I could not yet glean the refuse, so there was only one course. I searched until I found a bakery whose owner was arguing with the market manager over money. With shaking knees and a fluttering heart, I successfully committed my first theft.

I stole a string of sausages next. I thought I would take one, but it was linked to many others and the shopwoman saw her snake of red meat disappearing and I ran quickly away, trailing them after me. She cried out for my head, but I shuffled away into the crowd.

When I found a safe place by a pillar, I stopped and breathed hard, but there was voice behind me.

"You know, if you wait until closing, sometimes they'll give you that for free. Maybe help them clean up." He was the slightest slip of a boy, like me almost, had I been a boy, for he had thick black hair and a long face and nose, which would look handsome and distinguished when he became a man. The only difference were his eyes, which were a deep green that seemed entirely out of place in that city. "Maybe you can tell them a story. You've written a lot of things, I bet."

226

"What is your name?"

"Merkus, lady friend. And yours?"

"Ada. Thank you for the advice. I assume you have had to use it."

"Yes, come, I'll show you."

After searching for someone to help, Merkus and I found an older dairyman and assisted him in loading and unloading milk buckets. I told him a story of a shoemaker who learned the secrets of Solomon's cobbler and so could make shoes that whisked the owner to anywhere in the world, but that in the daytime the leather cunningly folded itself into ordinary books and so hid themselves upon his shelf.

Elisha was the dairyman's name, and he liked the story and so gave us some milk in an old leather bottle. I swept out the stall of a fruit seller as she closed up and she gave me a few plums that were going soft.

Merkus and I walked to the Temple Platz and ate our feast of stolen sausages, bread, old plums and fresh milk underneath the statue of The Lady. Her arms were outspread over us, and there were several other indigents and travelers in the place, huddled together in the evening.

"This is neutral ground, you know. The City Guards consider it a sanctuary, and there is no in-thieving here either out of respect for The Lady. No one gets beaten up or raped here. It's a nice place to come at night or when you need to rest. Are you going to be in Spandau long?"

"No, I am leaving tomorrow for Jena. I have no money right now and I must go to the mail yard tonight. I do not want to miss the coach. Thank you for your wisdom today."

"Thank you for your company. It is free here, but it does get lonely, you know. It is too bad for the city you are leaving, but good for you."

He agreed to walk me back to the coach yard, and we sat there together as the darkness grew thicker and more kindly. We did not worry about the porters or guards. They had business of their own. Like a lost brother and sister, we sat together. We were in no magical forest, but only in a mail yard amongst piles of horse manure and the armies of beetles who clicked and clacked at their work. When the light failed, and I could mark the wheeling of the Great Wain above the northern roof of the world, I felt better. The gray humid clouds cleared away and the night had turned to ultramarine above the coach yard. The walls of stone contained a wide space under the dome of stars, and the darkened windows had emptied of their diurnal life.

"You know, we may not be in a fancy house, Ada, but we are free."

I wondered: How long will he be free? How long will he live? His head, lousy and tangled, was laying on me, and I realized it was the second time in a day a man had laid his head upon me. Modran had never done that. I stroked Merkus's head as he told me how he had gotten there. He was a lost boy from the farmlands outside of this city. Alone and illiterate.

I recalled all of Modran's rages, his points of disregard that widened out. I looked at one stone and realized it was partnered and intricately laid with many others, and such was the time I had known Modran, but I found myself still considering a single stone, not the pavement itself. Was not Merkus a stone that had helped me? I remembered the Indigo Man as well just then, and I realized the arms of mountains had sheltered me. How sheltered I had been. How lacking in empathy or any real knowledge.

I had conceived many mountains in my soul and piled them upon themselves. I capped them in snow with my own hand, for I wished to freeze the slopes against the snails and slugs who would devour the garden within myself. It did not occur to me that the garden was dying of thirst, so vigilant was I upon my battlements. Had I allowed any storms over the passes, I may have had the churn of rot and warm life growing in its own healthy compost, but my rarefied defenses, so open to the mysteries of clear, star-filled nights, held fast against any such incursion.

I had left the mountains and the shelter of high, dry places: of snow that does not melt but evanesces as the weather and seasons change. I walked down into mud, frog-body clumpings, lilacs, berries like red blood-blisters, the smell of milk, my own armpits and crotch, whitewash, crushed brick, horseshit, pastries, and alder smoke.

Merkus broke the silence: "Tell me another of your stories, Ada."

I thought of Hagen and its salt-spray and incessant rains. I missed the seagulls and the masts of ships, the great bonfires in summer upon the Circus, the Great Carnival that brought the world to the city. I looked up at the cold stars and watched their sidereal time and knew that exile is a bereavement from a place, a time—and so ourselves.

"Very well. Upon a time ..."

Hagen

...In a sunlit cellar, in the Free and Hanseatic City of Hagen, there lived a little girl who often played along upon a carpet. What came before the carpet? Well, the whole world, of course, but what the little girl really knew of first, for it stayed with her like a shadow or a friendly dog, was the carpet. It was a rich old Karock Rus carpet: a possession of her father's family that had somehow remained with him down through the years, through the loss of capital, lands, and titles. Her father often reminded her that the carpet had once graced rich and wealthy houses, and would again someday. Could she still play on it there, she had asked, but her father, who was a busy man, never seemed to answer her.

He lived upon the sea in a wooden house that moved around the world. It had trees and sheets for wings and was a beautiful thing upon the water. Her mother would hold her up to watch him leave upon the ship. These memories began after the carpet. She remembered when her tall father returned with his dark hair and long nose. And the little girl knew he was a tall man because he stood a head above all the other men, including her uncle. They did not have to stoop when coming in through the cellar door, but her father did.

In the best times, he held her in his lap and told her stories of Venelova and how she was clever and waited: how she made a compact with the queen of the mice, and how the Lord of the Ravens was her friend. He told her stories of Orthus, Venelova's husband, and how he was clever and wandered, always desiring to return home, yet blown off course by monsters, Gods, and sorceresses. Yet he had a special compass that always pointed to home, not north, and so he would return. He had promised.

The little girl believed in Venelova, because her own mother also sat at a loom: *clack-clack* it went. The little girl's uncle would often come and take the linen and wool to sell. And so the little girl's first memories set themselves amongst the long regularities of these days. The carpet extended an invitation to travel in warp and weft beyond the cellar, to meet the creatures and roads woven upon it.

Griffins and dragons flew over mountains and rivers, tigers and dreaming women lounged in gardens and lay beneath the stars on steppes. The little girl found pathways over the mountains and through their caverns. She marked where bridges lay broken or whole. She followed the trade routes across the wide places where manticores and phoenixes ate their feasts of fireberries and juiceruby fruits.

And at night she had other reasons to believe in Orthus; the cave of the one-eyed troll was very dark, and in that darkness he ate the other sailors. It would begin with an argument about money: gold from some dragon's hoard that remained unplundered. Sometimes it was silver from the brown-robed men. Sometimes it was copper from the distant South. Sometimes the little girl heard their cries in the darkness. Sometimes they wept and others they insistently cried out. It sounded hurtful—but of the deeper meaning, she could not tell. There would be punching sometimes, and biting, but most often just words whispered in the darkness. It ended when Orthus drove his ash-spear deep into the troll's eye. The troll's friends never seemed to believe him when he spoke out about it.

One day, the little girl's father left. It was early in the morning. He did not say goodbye to them. She heard him stirring: the sound of subtle feet in tiptoe boots and a coat put on. He breathed in the challenge of keeping the quiet and its peace. The little girl heard him. But she heard too late: when she padded into the carpet room, she saw only the shadow of his back; he left it for a moment in the brightened doorframe. She ran to it but the blank black plane of the door closed swiftly between them and clicked shut. When she opened it, he was gone into the enormous streets and oceans of the world.

 The little girl, the carpet, and her mother moved to a new cellar. It was not as bright and cheerful. It was not as large. The carpet climbed one wall a little and soot from the charcoal pan fell on it. There was not very much to eat. The Sun was a rare ghost in the little girl's mind. This cellar dug itself into the ground where it could hide in the shadows of houses around it. The girl could not see outside, for the windows were thick and not clear. There was mud on them from the street.

The little girl's mother was better at making fuss and would often declare aloud that the girl should be grateful there was light at all. The girl was not ungrateful. Although she listened to her mother, she paid closer attention to her own travels on the carpet. Her mother would often go back to bed, for she was tired from carrying around the individual who would become the little girl's sister.

The little girl's uncle came more often, for he was the brother of the girl's mother and cared about them. Sometimes he would take the girl out into the greater city: to the harbor where masts and booms thickly massed around the piers and where great treasuries of grain, salt, fish, silks, spices, ore, porcelain, timber, and jewels flooded out into the streets. Roma, Jews, Saxons, Hageners, Berbers, Finns, Russians, and Yorkmen all throbbed through the city, and with them their thousand tongues spoke and told thousands of stories in a delicious glottal river. She loved to listen to the languages and tongues and found she could repeat them even better than her uncle.

And they often went to visit The Lady beneath the great blue dome of Her temple. Once it was timber framework filled with a mixture of rubble, and daub. Later it was made of stone and brick. It had always been home to The Lady, and the little girl liked it best in the quiet afternoons there.

The Lady's hair was long and black, painted by the night—it seemed—so that it shone like jet. Her clothes glowed gold like the harvests and were made from the melted cups and coins of monkery mummers. In the winter, the little girl went with her uncle to celebrate the Longest Night: the Night when Her dark was even and endless and She bid the snow to fall, until it was empty of dreams and the clouds cleared so the stars could glitter red and blue in reflection upon the alb of the Earth. The Lady stood beneath Her dome with one eye closed. Some say it was a blind eye to suffering, or an eye given to learn the secrets of the world.

Going outside into the cold, clear night—the Longest Night—the little girl asked her uncle why The Lady's eye was closed.

Her uncle said, "I don't know. Our Father possesses but one eye as well. But The Lady taught Him much: that we know."

But the little girl, who looked somewhat like the Lady, liked to think it was all a joke.

"I get it," she said. "She is winking at me. The others do not see this."

"I hope you are right."

"Uncle, what are the stars?" she asked.

"Each star is someone's dream. That is why they rekindle in the night. Do not fear the morning or the clouds. They will be there in the evening. Is it not a comfort to look up and see the dreams are still there?"

"Where is mine?"

"You will have to look for it, and so make that star."

As she grew, her father never returned. Part of her came to know that he did not go to war and was not captured by Spanish pirates. He had simply grown tired of them and their hold on him, so he abandoned them. Yet part of her still traveled over the carpet and imagined it the great garden of her future, full of the smell of lavender water on drying clothes. She could see the smile of her daughter at the recognition of the Moon. On some rainy day in the yet-to-be, she would sit near a real window and consider the memories of her father whom she would never see again. Yet sometimes she considered finding him, traveling to the far mountains. There, she would see griffins and tigers. Perhaps she would speak with a dragon.

Her uncle taught the girl her first letters, for he was always impressed with how good she was with words and languages. It seemed as though she could understand the traders even better than him. But this did not make her happy, for whenever she looked up, the basement window was thick and dingy from the rain and mud. All was gray, diffuse, and plain. There were no shadows in the brief winter days, save only for the night which was the greatest shadow of them all. Sometimes she played with her little sister upon the floor, but the girl—now quite tall for her age, though skinny—grew weary of her younger sibling. The little sister always needed taking care of. Sometimes she tried to eat nails or beetles. The little girl knew the baby couldn't help it, and so she cleaned up her sister's filth and made sure she ate on the days when their mother would remain in the bed like a stone. The girl's sister did not seem to understand the importance of the carpet and often interrupted the girl when she was reading.

The days went unto years for quite some time, until the day after her eighth birthday, she was given a choice. Her uncle and her mother both sat down and looked at her in the yellow light of the pork-oil lamp.

"She will never be a good weaver," her uncle said, "but that is not what she was made for."

"What will I do? I must have help," her mother said.

"She will be tall and strong like her father, I've no doubt."

"You mean tall and skinny. There is no question she is his child. She will always be Elsewhere," her mother said.

Her uncle looked sad when she said this. "But if she goes

to the Library, she can travel all over the world in books and be close to us," he added.

"That kind does not raise a family."

"Yes they do."

"They do not speak with their old mothers once they cross that threshold."

"Some of them do."

"We are not rich; how do you propose we send her there?"

"She will pass the exams; I have no question about that. *Ita quod non est? Exaudi me in English.*"

"It is so," the girl said in perfect Danelaw English.

"Maybe you can talk to her father's family," her mother said.

"I already have and they have made the arrangements."

"Really? Then what are you asking me any of this for? She is as much your daughter as mine it seems. Maybe more so. What are you really doing? Raising her to be your clerk?"

And though the uncle and mother argued, it was decided that the girl, who as I have said was quite tall and smart—albeit skinny and not particularly pretty—went to become an Apprentice in the Library.

Flood-carried and tangle-haired, the girl felt like a ship-wrecked sailor, flopped upon the steps of the Library. It did not take long, perhaps a day, to wander into the vast forest of books. There were books about places and peoples and their languages and books about memories that the languages preserved. They spoke of everything from spinning tops to fire giants to the thousands of varieties of government in China. The Great Library contained thousands upon tens of thousands of books, and all manner

of people came and went to look upon them and learn—to copy something, perhaps—or look up the latest news in New Amsterdam or even New Hagen on the far side of the western continents. She first worked in the Library press itself, which was famous across the world. She swept the dust and scrap-rags, and tended the smelting fires for the print. She fetched ink for the pressman and even learned to read upside down and backwards, but she hid this from her masters. While she admired their skill and art, she did not wish to reproduce the words of others. She wanted to take care of the language and memories and so graduated into classes that concerned various languages, their writing systems. She also learned the mathematics used to keep the large and unwieldy catalog in shape although it was a never ending task, like making a rope out of sand. She and the other students, mostly girls, learned how important it was to care for the books, the scrolls, the papers, and the languages, for Hagen was the Alexandria of the North, and never could they let the fire of unreason again put out the eye of wisdom.

The girl grew—as though she ate books—but she did not make many friends. Most of the other children were from different families, richer. She was poorer and though she was smarter than most of them; this made enemies, mostly, along with a few usurious friends who turned their backs once tests were over.

"Her father wasn't a captain. I think he was a second mate."

"Then he wasn't lost at sea?"

"No, he probably sailed across it between some other whore's legs."

In whispers, "I think you are nice, but I can't really talk to you anymore."

The end of her chances at joining the greater flower of girlhood ended on a day when she was running errands for the circulators. When a request for a book came in, they would send the girl to fetch it. She was like a spider: silent, swift, and long legged. She always seemed to know where to go, but one day an obscure book by an Italian artist was missing. She searched and searched for it. So nervous was she about returning empty handed that she continued to search the other shelves, ignoring the time and ignoring her bladder, which painfully insisted on capitulation. No. There was another place. It has been mis-shelved, she told herself. I think it is over here.

She was right, but it was too late. Not two seconds after putting it in the hand of the circulator, the girl peed herself right there—yes, behind the main circulation desk. Because it was the heart of the Library, the news circulated. Never very popular, she was the Piss Girl now, and was shunned by everyone, save a few other outcasts.

She continued her studies and shrank even further into herself. She learned Greek so that she could read the *Iliad*, which the boys favored, but she preferred the *Odyssey*, for there at last was the first version of *Venelova and Orthus*. Even then the girl did not understand why Odysseus remained so long with Circe and Calypso. Why did he not return home?

The mornings became her sacred time: before the rest of them were awake, when Night, indifferent and therefore beautiful, went to sleep in the red flush of dawn. She could see the Elbe running out to the sea: the Elbe, the Holy Mother of Hagen itself and Her universal waters fascinated the girl with all of its deep and hidden secrets. The sea breezes would come and steal over the girl, bearing the scent ghosts of the ocean: the fish, the weeds, the creosote of the pilings and the soft-fleshed animals translucently sinking. The salt froth and the water came in mists and fogs and it was like the breath of the gods.

It was an autumn morning such as that when she became a woman, with no one but the early Sun and the sleeping Night to celebrate with. Never in the right time, it seemed then. She was supposed to wait for spring like the other girls so that they could don the crown of red candles, wear a shower of cherry blossom petals in their hair and dresses, and bring the cherry-laden jam breads to their families on the first day of Ostara. But the girl rarely visited her family, and she was never going to be a Cherry Blossom Daughter. She merely found some rags and awkwardly put them between her legs, as she had read of in books about the subject.

So it was to her surprise when Rolf, the handsome son of a bookseller, took an interest in her four years later as she neared the end of her apprenticeship, just before her collegiate matriculation. Rolf was blonde and handsome, descended of Norse raiders, but softened by Time and Civilization into the beautiful figure of a bookseller's son. He had a proud shine in his eyes, the same conquering surety of the Sun. He saw the young woman and he smiled. That was when it started.

The young woman smiled when she found a pot of flowers on her desk: muslin-red tulips from Anatolia that yearned open for the young woman in twelve fleeting cups: twelve mouths of space, twelve moments of delicate pistils and stamens. The young woman read deeply into their carmine metaphor. Dawdling at her studies, she drew clumsy pictures of him in the middle of her tablets. She entwined her name with his around these pictures. He came to call on her, and distracted her at the most wonderfully worst of times, usually before exams or during some important chore for a senior librarian. Always there was a reproaching, silent glance, for that was the manner in which all the librarians spoke to one another. The young woman felt herself wishing to laugh aloud as his eyes smiled and mocked the librarian.

It was therefore only a matter of time before the young couple found a more permissive silence together in the Library. He playfully followed her back to an old storeroom. There was broken furniture and hard bricks in secret darkness when he kissed her lips, kissed the soft hollow on her neck, kissed her eyes. She felt smooth and beautiful, but she did not know herself, did not know the world or what to do—until he pressed himself into her. The shock was complete. It came without warning, and brought no pleasure, only surprise. She grasped at a broken chair, felt him quicken, and it was done. She turned to strike him, so that he would know this: the young woman knew what it was they had done, but that was not how she had wished it to be. Had he no patience, had he no manners? Had—

And the librarian was there. Her arms were crossed. She sneered.

"As the best student, you know this is not allowed in this place; why could you have not gotten some shack or jakes to slake your lust in?" There were others, old classmates in the darkness. They tittered and snickered. Rolf pulled up his pants with pride and walked through them, but the young woman was now shamed.

Rolf disappeared from her life, for he was betrothed to a paper merchant's daughter. It was then that the young woman understood Odysseus: how he used Calypso and Penelope; how he left both of the women alone on separate beaches.

"You may work in the kitchens. You were never a good cook, but we cannot allow you into the main sections with this sort of turpitude about you. No, you will not be a librarian, but you may stay here with them."

The young woman went to her uncle.

"Your mother is not well."

"I know that."

"There is a way out of this. You do not need to work as a scullery maid. Every day will be an insult to you."

"They may change their minds; I'm sure it has happened before."

"That does not mean they will change their minds."

"What do you suggest?"

"Have you thought of the family business?"

"Weaving? I don't know how to weave."

"It's not weaving itself, but perhaps marrying someone who does."

And her uncle arranged a marriage, as was done among the burgers of the city. The young woman would marry a rich cloth merchant who would take care of the young woman's mother and sister. The young woman would be his third wife, for he was old and fat. His first wife had given him children, and he made his fortune off the solid investment of her dowry before she died of fever. The second wife was beautiful and he had loved her, but she had died in childbirth. As the third wife, the young woman was expected to raise the children of the first two wives. He would give her some children as well, he promised, for he fancied her skin and hair, but they would never inherit any of the property, of course, owing to her family's low standing.

Her uncle did not approve of this, exactly, but it was all he could manage. Her uncle was not a very important man, and they both knew it.

"Have you spoken with my father's family about this?" the young woman asked.

"I have tried, but my messages were not answered."

"Tell me, I am of their blood. Where may I find them?"

The young woman's distant family lived on estates somewhat outside the city. They were descended from the old Hun aristocracy who had assumed power after the tumult and fall of the Roman Empire. They had welcomed the Julian exiles just as they had welcomed the exchanged brides and grooms from the Great Khan's empire, and while the growth of the cities and commerce and learning had continued, the smarter of these aristocrats kept their lands and wealth. But as with anything under the Sun, changes occur. While the famed raven clout hair and milk-tea skin of the Hagen aristocracy could still be found, it was not as exclusive as it once was. Some members became estranged from the greater families, and so it was with the young woman's father. His family had not been part of nobility for two generations, yet they remained on friendly, if subordinate terms.

This is why it was no great surprise to have a penniless pauper woman be allowed an audience with a great, powerful (and wealthy) graffin. Like the young woman's father, the Graffin was quite tall, and she bore the long nose the family was also known for.

"Yes, so you are family," the older woman said. "Our blood runs true and strong—of that there is no doubt. I have some knowledge of what you are here for."

The young woman was glad of the manners she had been taught at the Library and sat on a low stool, deferentially looking down the whole time. They spoke of weather and pleasantries at first, but then the Graffin pressed her hard. There would be no charity.

"Your father's family cheated their way out of that, and you know by now that that is true and incontrovertible. I cannot hide you here and break a marriage contract, for that would be against the city code, and they would jump at any chance to confiscate our business holdings here, especially that damned Eldredsohn and his son. Yet somehow I do not think that is why you are here. So tell me, I am intrigued: what do you want?"

"To go elsewhere, and I must ask for charity to do so. I do

not need money, but I do need to know what to do. I would rather die than lie under that fat old—"

"I understand," she interrupted. "I was fortunate to be the eldest child—and the strongest—and so inherited the title and estates or the same might have happened to me."

The Graffin looked at the young woman for quite some time and finally said:

"You write well? They must have taught you that at the Library."

"Yes, madam, I—"

"Give me your hand."

The young woman did so and the Graffin studied it, turning it over and over. "It will be a very pretty purple hand. You say you do not ask for money, but you are asking for charity. I offer no charity, but I will offer you employment somewhere far away. Our family owns shares in a mining concern in the Harz Mountains, and I understand they are in need of a scribner-clerk. I can get you into the Scribner's Guild with a letter, but it means you will bear the purple hand the rest of your days."

The day before she was to meet the merchant at the town hall for marriage, the young woman packed only a few things, such as an old Harsager book and a Fisherman's Sweater that was very much like her father's. Her mother and sister were still asleep, and she silently walked out the door of the old cellar—straight into her uncle.

He studied her closely.

"You are taller than I am. You are like your father, you know. Did you know that I admired him greatly, once?"

"Once?"

"You will learn it is different when you clean up someone

else's mess. And you will, but for now there is that spark of courage and adventure that I always admired in him. Here. Here's some money." She threw her arms around him and kissed him. Then he told her goodbye.

"For I do not think I will see you again."

The young woman met the purple-handed clerk of the Graffin before the doors of an appointed Fosthorpe Tattooery. The clerk was there to make sure everything happened as arranged. It was a long process and involved just the right amount of Schnapps and Opium for the young woman to endure a complete tattoo of her hand: from fingertips to just past the wrist, palm and all. The tattooist, who had done this many times for the guild, asked the young woman:

"What mark would you like?"

The young woman looked at the scribner.

"Your seal will need to be the same," she said. "That way they'll know it is you."

The young woman had seen three swallows outside the man's shop. As the opium began to take effect, she remembered them swooping and diving. Their flight was so swift and effortless. "Swallows, three swallows."

"Very nice. Now, I am afraid this will be extremely painful. I will continue if you pass out. That usually happens with the fingertips. Are the straps too tight? And yes, I'm afraid lying face down is the best way. You won't choke on you vomit from the opium. Can you move your hand just a bit? If you can take some more, I recommend another sip."

Something We Fall Through

"The carpet was your first metaphor. The little girl was you. Why do you speak of yourself like you weren't you? You did not say 'I' to that boy or me."

"The story of I is first person, but history is often written in the third person."

"Who is the second person?"

"You."

Anton laughs. "I understand you better now," he says. Anton relaxes his shape, beginning to take off the red woman's skin as though it was stockings and a blouse. The skin hangs for a moment in his claws, but it does not drip blood. It merely becomes transparent and then disappears. He notices my attention.

"Yes, it disappears, just like your lives and all the different masks you wear. You are alone as I am upon this mountain, Ada. You searched for this Modran so you could hate him. But you also hate your father? I can understand that. It seems fairly common amongst your kind, so much so that I would say the role of a father is to be loved and hated at the same time. And yet you all wish for your fathers."

"That is not true. I have learned in my time upon this earth the answer to that old laziness: the bitter words of disappointed men who seek the quick and reassuring phrases of ignorance. I believed it myself for a while. Yet though I have traveled far, it was my own city that finally provided me the answer."

"Hagen is a place bound up in money; we breathe avarice and inhale greed. The mode of exchange must be familiar. Something the merchant or banker can count on. Love is also a metal from which the currency of exchange is made. It's why coins have two sides, both marked with runes, perhaps a face on one side, ringed with annotations of cruelty, disregard and jealousy, wrath and resentment. On the inverse side are symbols of affection and grace, trust and respect. The coin flies and flips through our lives if we allow it and yet we always wish for the coin to stay the same. Exchange for some foreign coins is hard, and we fear the rates will betray us. So we seek, and desire, and keep the money that we know—even if it's to purchase some rope."

"It seems the same to me," Anton says.

"Because you are not inside—here." I point to my heart. "If you must know, I did not hate my father for leaving me; it was that he did not take me with him. The difference is subtle, but it lived with me until—"

"Until that man came whistling into your life."

"Thirteen years ago I desired to be in a 'now' that never really was, or an 'if' that never really could be."

"Are they the same ghost, but living on opposite sides of a most smoky mirror? Your memory is faulty, and a bad memory is the strange guard the gods placed on the doorway of human dignity, a senile wolf who faces both ways. Throughout this night I have wondered: How can you remember all of this so clearly? Perhaps you are just making it up."

"It was a long time ago, but I remember."

"I do not know what a long time is to you. I am not even sure I understand what you mean by time."

"It is something we fall through. We are never sure from where we fell, but we know that we are falling to the earth."

"Strange. But that still does not answer my question. How can these memories be so clear to your daylit mind?"

"Do you not taste these memories, in the full richness of their savor, when you eat one of my kind?"

"Yes."

"That is why. It is all I can say. Our daylit minds are small, Anton, but our bodies contain oceans of memories."

"Oh."

"And if those memories are of strong emotion, such as great injury or love or both, then they can remain fresh until the day we die."

"Was this the first time you could speak the truth? To someone you did not know? You had lied to your lover about pregnancy driving you out of your home city."

"I had to start somewhere, Anton. For all its man-hewn clumsiness, for the filth upon the ground and the articulations of the beetles, I felt at peace in the carriage yard, and thankful such emotions could still live. For in its emptiness of people and daylight, I could only see the living ghosts of dreams and desires moving about the wide space. We all had somewhere to go, and many of us were late at finding it, I thought. The general disregard—the indifference of the world was not to blame, but only explained. At last I felt a part of the world's indifference, the contained space we all occupy that will be forgotten, disregarded, and therefore allowed to live.

"As the stars turned above me on that courtyard, I asked them a question: 'If someone cares enough to hate, doesn't that still remain a care? I have long sought for that. No, that is a childish thing to wish for: the hand that beats, the mouth that spits. Let me choose my concerns and indifferences carefully now, for they will follow me like newly hatched goslings.'"

I had a few silver pennies left and I put them in Merkus's pocket.

"Thank you, Ada. May The Lady watch your road."

In the morning, Merkus was gone. I felt a single kiss on my lips and I knew it was him, yet I could not climb fast enough out of the mines of my sleep. By the time I reached the dawn, he was gone.

The first hostler had brought out a team of horses and was hitching them. He looked at me.

"Are you the one bound out for Jena?"

"Yes."

"This will be your coach. Your friend left; I would suggest checking to see what he has stolen from you."

But Merkus had not stolen anything. My seal and pens, which he could have stolen and sold, were there. He had need of nothing and I was glad for to have given him what little money I had left of Spandau. It was a small price, for I would have traded a thousand memories of Modran's first appearance on the mountain to have said goodbye to Merkus. I stood up and wrapped my hair in the scarf. I knew my second life was done and that the third was not going to

be some idyll on that liar's arm. Whatever my third life was
going to be, it lay before me, so I went forth into it. I went to
sit down at one of the communal tables. I had a few pennies

for tea and ate the rest of the stale bread and milk from the night before.

After breakfast I waited for the morning clerk to return to the office. I wondered if it was going to be Friedrich and if he would look at me differently. Would he smile? No, probably pretend nothing. Perhaps a sneer? But the morning clerk was different and she handed me a large sealed envelope sealed by Friedrich.

Scribner and Notary Ludenow: you are now bound to service to the Emperor for such needs as he sees fit in the space of four years. Along with the message was a small, plain seal bearing only the crown of the Emperor along with a number: 876. There were no swallows, nor did it bear my name, for such was the practice when a Hanseatic scribner entered the service of the Emperor. I would keep using my Hagen seal, but I would stamp, in black ink, this supplementary seal upon documents as was necessary. There were some shillings for traveling expenses, I supposed, along with a letter of mark for the rest of my commission. This was most precious, for it would be my life-money for four years. Fortunately, I could only draw it in quarters or other smaller amounts; I presume this was to keep me from losing it. Or worse: investing it and making some money off the Emperor.

I then wrote out a letter to the captain of the City Guards indicating who my traveling companion had been and whom he was with in Spandau should the Guards wish to question him about his affairs in the Harz Mountains. I posted it with the clerk, went outside, and climbed into the coach. I knew it was early morning, for the Sun was not yet above the rooftops as I left Spandau.

"Yet by my count that means you had thirteen turns of the Sun between then and now? Are you still looking for the man? Yes, that is why you returned here. That *is* a long answer to the riddle."

"I could not know that the riddle would be so far and so long."

Return to Visingotha

Leaving Spandau, I did have some desire to see Modran. I was still young and I wished to enact revenge on him or at least get some of my money back. You do not need to point out that foolishness to me, so close your mouth and listen: what would I have done had I had my money? I was alone in a strange city. In the coach, I did dream of the money, and perhaps paying a gang of cutthroats to do their work on his cock and balls and so rid the world of three nuisances. Would I have enough for his tongue and all his pretty fingers as well? At some point I realized my accounting of his body parts was pointless, since I was poor and on the way to Jena. And yet I was not on the way to Jena so quickly, for Doktor Kreidler waylaid me yet again.

He was amused at my situation:

"It appears you have even less now than before. A few shillings and a piece of paper? Where is your bank, Ms. Scribner? I mean both the financial one and your mounte."

The pun was terrible, but I could not help but smile. "And your monthly condition is upon you again."

Thanks to that and a display of my incumbent powers, they let me live without raping or murdering me, or murdering then raping me, or whatever combination they could have dreamed up. Kreidler considered me a valuable source of information on the movement of money, and so I remained in their service. They were more generous with food than the mining company had been, and Kreidler was a much more agreeable manager. Yet the days of roast venison and wine came to an end when the Water's habitual lack of clarity led to a massacre of the men. I had thought the herd of pigs I saw was symbolic, but they were sadly literal and confused and made a havoc of a robbery in time for a troop of the Emperor's Guards to arrive. Thanks to "a safe distance," which Kreidler taught me to observe and observe from, we escaped. I feared it would be the end of me, but instead he surprised me by granting me my freedom. He had been considering retirement for a long time anyway, and I had done him a good turn by vastly reducing the number of shareholders in his enterprise. But he had one last trick, or favor: a black eye and a push into a ravine.

When I was captured, my appearance fooled the Guards enough to let me go, although I was informed that my service to the Emperor had been considered "on hold" during that time because I had never been given a commission as an officer of the law.

I thought of returning to Visingotha at that point. I made toward the mountains, but I somehow overshot them and wound up in the Rhine Palatinate, scribbling letters and making myself useful in that strange land where Protestant

Christians fought with Catholic ones, and the members of the Old Religion kept a wary eye on all of them.

I traveled to England in the service of the Emperor and made friends with some of the actors and playwrights there: an impressive bunch of fellows, although somewhat given over to buggery and bar fights. They thought I was a boy at first, owing to the manner of my dress and their overused theatrical devices. One balding fellow wrote a number of poems for me even after he discovered I was a woman. We were lovers for a time, and I learned a trick or two of writing from him as we lay in bed. And he is right. My dark eyes are nothing like the sun.

For a time I gave up the pursuit of Modran, for I wished to return to Hagen. Near the end of my commission in England, the Council of Hagen called for scribners, and I thought I had a chance of at least returning home. I had some money saved now in a bank in Rotterdam, but I was instead sent to the Kingdom of France to work as a secretary for the ambassador. I met a young, handsome bishop at court named Armand Jean. He was much shorter than I was, but he loved learning and philosophy. Although we enjoyed our lovemaking and the long arguments over monotheism that followed, I thought him overly fond of cats and he did not fancy the dramatic difference in our height. He was a bishop though, and I was only a heathen scribner, so we both knew our love was going to be short. I left Paris and considered once again returning here, to these mountains.

There were other strange adventures—not all of them occurring in this world—but when I finally returned to Hagen, it was very brief. Once again, I was deflected, this time by conscription into the service of an expedition of natural philosophy leaving from Norway. We traveled in a leaking boat across the North Atlantic, and I survived by eating raw sheep that had somehow putrefied in a magical way. Later I learned the Icelanders have somehow turned the food of desperation into a national cuisine—alas, what I ate wasn't very unusual at all. We traveled to chart the lands between the Northwest Passage and the Anischauven Lands to the south in the western continents. I saw great rivers—so broad they make the Elbe look like a stream in a gutter—and trees so vast and tall that a whole village could be built from one of them. It was from New Hagen on the western coast that we sailed then for the Japans and Cathay. It was there I—

"Yes, yes, yes, but did you ever find Modran?"

"No. I did not, though I sometimes heard rumor of him. But it always turned out to be some similar liar, tricking people and stealing other money. My knowledge of confidence-men and cheats became encyclopedic in my search, but I later surmised that they are really all the same person.

"But you returned here somehow."

"It was from the East. Since you don't wish for that particular tale, I will hold it for you in my library of thoughts, but yes, I returned via the Silk Road, or what was left of it and across the wide steppes where the tea caravans once ruled. Now that Hagen's ships carry her tea, the caravan routes are empty of all but the wind and the old tales it bears."

I returned from Russia and finally decided to come here to the Harz Mountains to see if I could find him—or at least find answers. Ever had I seen the nightingale, the stone, the pool and the tree in my dreams, and I had to return to them one last time. So much time had passed that I was unsure any of it had happened the way I remembered. It was strange retracing my journey across the Elbe's plain. Earlier, I had been lost in the myopic airs of love, but in the clarity of maturity, the Moonlight and the Sun revealed familiar fields and streams. The journey was not without specific sorrows.

I learned that a year after my visit, a gang of drunken roughs—brave men indeed—had gone out and murdered the indigo man after too much beer, too much boasting, too much wrath. I found a clothweaver; she whispered that they no longer made blue clothing. I looked around the town, wondering who of the brave drunks was now mayor.

"Tell me, were none of them punished?" I had asked.

The woman looked away and I had my answer, but a voice of urgency and discreetness said to me: "Not all of the town was for it, miss."

Someone stood by the stable door. At first I did not mark him. He was a man, ruddy-faced like any other, of an age I could not determine. He had a crooked nose. His eyes could not agree on a single point of gaze. His hat was battered.

"Some that weave will miss him. We'll have no blue here anymore. And why?"

"Why?" I asked, approaching him.

"Why indeed. Why do boys pull the wings off small beautiful things like butterflies? Because they can, miss. I know I was a boy once, and now I'm just here. Old and unmarried. A hobbled leg, cut off by accident—this boot is filled with wood. I am as much a part of this door, I suppose. I could go on and on. The world ain't a kind place. Somehow I think you know that. You look sad, miss. You should be, because few else here are sad for him. I am, but no one cares.

But I want you to know that not all of us who live here like what they did. When will I be next? That's what I wonder, and then I wonder, *Why bother with it all?* I could just as soon tip myself over that well there and be done with it. Why do I go on? Why do you?"

"That is something I cannot answer. It has been in my heart, but not my head. Thank you." I walked away from him.

Nona had died in Bärenburg, and none there remembered me. I did not stay in that inn. I was not given over to such nostalgia—yet. It was warm and I stood naked, as I had so long before when Modran slept, retracing my steps to that night.

The next day I could not mark the spot where Modran and I had made love by the brook, perhaps for the last good time, but I remembered it well enough. In Askanleben I learned that I was still wanted for assisting in the murder of Von Duschter.

This fact—that Von Duschter was dead and Modran had something to do with it—hung in my thoughts all the way up the mail road until the old coach of the Emperor dropped me and my old rucksack off at the crossroads inn of Visingotha. It looked magically different and I first wondered what magic had occurred. I had become accustomed to strange things. Then I realized it was simply the very ordinary magic of prosperity: in this case its signature trick was a coat of whitewash and corresponding respectability. I would not be staying there, of that I knew. I had long planned this return and I did not wish to have any shred of criminality stop me.

I had learned a few tricks.

I took the dust of the road and water from the little brook that ran by it and muddied my face. In the Water I saw vague spaces that had been my old home and I knew something had changed there and I wished to see what had happened. I put on another old and battered brown dress. I tied my hair up in a scarf, put a ragged mitten over my hand, and festooned my rucksack with ribbons. I hunched over as far as I could and walked the road into town under the evening sky.

Nightingales still sang there and the sky was kindly; it sparkled with stars again in the clear air and I found the old pathways as surely as anything, for this was home—of sorts. I wanted very much to see my cabin, to perhaps look once more in the pool and see if the tree still stood in its melancholy watch. I walked past where the old mining office had been; a new building of stone and half timbers stood on the spot and spoke of a new infusion of money. The town square was now paved in stone.

The old pathway from the town to my house was empty save for a few miners, none of whom I recognized. I remembered that they had been but children when I left Visingotha. I walked by a new ore-crushing mill and even newer shaft houses. A sluice ran next to the road and I followed it. The sky was an early September sky, deep sapphire, and it was clear, like my memories of Modran that first night.

Someone was outside the old cabin, though now it had an addition built onto the front of it. I slowed and stopped. A man was speaking low and someone was standing near him. There was a child in his arms. They all looked up to the heavens, to where the man was pointing out stars.

"There is the Wain, and the end of it points toward the pole star of the North. And there is the Great Dragon wrapped around it. He sees us, little one. Will he come down? No, because, you see, the Hammer of the Gods is just there, as a warning. Hello, can I help you, ma'am? I'm afraid we don't need any ribbons. Are you lost?"

"In a manner of speaking."

"There is nothing that way, ma'am."

But I kept going, leaving them silhouetted against the light of the cabin. I walked along the sluicework and wept, for then I guessed the purpose it served.

A great hole was in the ground where my pool had been. The stone had been wrenched from the earth and where it was, I could not know. The fir tree had been cut down and was perhaps one of the timbers holding up the sluicework. The sluice carried the spring water down the hill toward the mine. Only the nightingale remained, hidden somewhere, save only for its song that seemed far sadder than I had ever heard. Everything was gone. I thought of Modran, of my stupidity and wishes for a family with him. The cabin now possessed a family, like a Djinn-wish with all of the twisting jokes of fate.

There were only ghosts upon that mountain. Above the cabin, and toward the peak and the old mine, I could still perceive them winding, forever, along the path to the mouth of the earth that swallowed them. I returned to Visingotha.

I banged on the familiar door, although it was late. I had nowhere else to go.

"Sir."

"We have no alms, sister—Ada, what!? Please, come in!"

Benjamin pulled me into his shop and closed the shutters.

He doused all but one candle and sat me by the hearth with a mug of tea and a basin in which to wash.

"I do not think I will," I said, smiling. "I am not afraid of the water anymore. I just don't want to lose my disguise."

· "Your disguise did not fool me, but then again I am somewhat accustomed to your feet." He looked down. "Barefoot is a good idea," he said, laughing. He was gray in his beard and temples now. A little heavier, a little more bent, but his eyes still sparkled blue and gray. "I think I am the only one who would recognize those long feet of yours. The rest, I will say, did fool me. Where are the shoes?" He did not say this harshly but with a strange enthusiasm.

"I think you know already, Benjamin. We parted ways in Elsewhere. Cathay, specifically."

We laughed at this. He had much to ask, and I had much to say. I told him some of my journey, but I had to compress vast spaces and times of the earth.

"Well, that is a tale. I mean, the rest of it is fantastic, something out of a book, you know. Thieves, poets, Cathay! When are you writing it down? That is what I wish to know. I won't live forever, you know. Still, I am just glad you are not dead, but I shouldn't speak too soon. May all the angels watch over you. You know that technically you are still a wanted woman here."

"I was never that before, here."

"Ha, ha. Perhaps that is what you thought then, but I will not engage in ribald talk with a traveler such as yourself. You will overmatch me, but I knew that man was no good. Are you really going to try to find him? That is a stupid question. I know you—of course you are. That may have been a stupid question, but your quest is a stupid one."

"I want my money back."

"It's not the money. You and I know this."

"No. I tried to tell that to others and none of them believed me either."

"My brother-in-law's sheep would not believe you. What is it that you seek, then?"

"I am not really sure anymore. For a while it was money, Benjamin. And then I wanted an answer. Why he did it. To have him tell me the truth for once. Just once."

"Ada, for a man like that, you will never have the truth, for the truth does not live in a golem made of lies. They are stronger than those made of rock or clay. You can hide here during the day and then leave under the cover of night, God willing."

"I am putting you in danger."

"Do not think of that. I will do the worrying over that. Lady Von Duschter and many of her servants still live here. Schröder died a few years ago, but the new director and a few others here would remember that height of yours. And that beautiful hair. You haven't aged a day."

"And you are a terrible liar."

"Well, that's true, at least, but I think this age suits you. Now go to sleep."

I slept soundly on a pile of rags in the back of his shop. I breathed deeply of the leather, the old skin of the cows he worked into shoes, and thought of the grass that fed them, the sky that sheltered them. I wanted to fly there and leave the earth, but sleep came upon me and I flew until the blue sky gave way to darkness of night and then black, dreamless sleep.

"What are you doing here, you fool!" It was Helga. She

rushed in, with Benjamin following her. She bore a basket covered with a blanket, which I found to hold bread, sausage, and wine.

As quietly as she could, Helga swore at me for quite a long time. Her profanity was impressive, for I had seldom heard her use it, and never in the expanse and intricacy she had reserved for me. When she was done, I retold the story again as the day wore on and we ate the sausage and bread and drank the wine. She sat closer and closer, grabbing my knee whether I was telling of wandering in Spandau like a beggar or clambering down a mountain pass near Wudan. I told her that I wished to go unto the far valley beyond the saddle of the hills and see if Modran's family lived there. She combed my hair, trimmed the ragged fringe above my eyes, and told me the story of Modran, how he had been the lover of Lady Von Duschter.

"It is not pleasant. From what I understand, Von Duschter discovered them together in love and flew into a rage. He was going to kill Modran, but Modran was faster. From what I have heard, he did not mean to kill Von Duschter. At least from what the hallward told me. He threw a vase at the man while he was trying to escape, and Von Duschter fell down the stairs of his hall and broke his neck. After that, his wife claimed Modran had raped her, although why she was naked and perfumed—with my own attar of orange—she could not say. Or rather she *would* not say. That's probably why you had just enough time to get away. The inquest called it murder. They named you as an accomplice, although the hallward said he had never seen you, only heard a rumor that you were Modran's other lover."

"Other lover." My laugh was faint, the sort that barely

cloaks sorrow.

"You had the misfortune of leaving with him. Still, there are some good things. Lady Von Duschter has invested her husband's money in the mine."

"I have seen that."

"You are going to weep? Do not weep for her."

"I am not. I cannot weep for Von Duschter. I would only weep at my own stupidity. How everything was a lie. I understand why Jorgi left us. He was paid off, no doubt."

"I am sorry, Ada. I am not trying to rub salt into the sores you have earned. Told-you-so's are not medically useful, I believe, although there are many here who live upon them like opium. What will you do?"

"I have told you," I said. I cried and could say little else.

"What about after you have gone to the Densingthal— that's what it's called, you know. You will find nothing there. You will not find him there. There is only a dilapidated hall where a shepherdess lives."

"How do you know this?"

"Her husband, Willi Dörscher, sometimes comes into the village for medicines. He has told me."

She was probably right. In yet another trick, my mind had never really questioned the validity of this belief in the Modral hall. Yet somehow I knew there was something there. Helga sensed this.

"The Water has shown you an answer, has it not?"

"A long time ago, in the Elbe I believe."

"The answer will only lead to other questions. But you are far stronger than I ever expected, although I knew you possessed a great strength. You are lucky. You have traveled. It was always what you were meant to do, ever since you were that little girl playing on the carpet in the cold cellar.

Just do not forget me. Find some place of refuge for a while. Go back to Hagen, perhaps, and if you write this out, put me in your tale somewhere. At least this time you shall say farewell to me."

And so the evening fell upon Visingotha. I left Helga and Benjamin again, waddling under my beggar woman's clothes. But I had new boots from Benjamin. I cried all the way out of town, so perhaps the townspeople just thought I was going off homeless: to find some hole to die in. It was not terribly far from what I feared was the truth. They did not care. As the evening deepened into night, I found myself quite alone on the spur path leading up to the Densingthal.

"Where is the proof of my love? How may I know it? Was it a lie, or a truth that became a lie upon discovery? Speak now, Wild. A place where there are no others save we in the dark."

I found comfort in my own conversation, as I always had. When the Wain had circled halfway in the night, I stopped. The summer evening was cooler, but I was hot from my labors up the mountain. At the entrance, I found a patch of firwood and bracken. The stream at the bottom of the dale ran over granite rocks into pools beneath a thicket of willows, and it was there that I finally removed the old dress and bathed.

I kept my eyes closed, but the water was so shocking, so cold, that I gasped and felt the life in me turn to ice, the old bones of the world. I had learned to love this feeling in the Great Mountains, and there I welcomed the visions coming through the sight of my skin and muscles. I saw mountains, new and hungry, rising through the clouds in order to drink of them. Yet it would be their long death, for the armies of clouds welcomed the mountains and a river grew and cut through them, running to the sea.

Upon the traveler's stage of my mind, reason was a small puppet who attempted to answer the question: "What is real?" I had learned the Water never spoke in equivalencies, but only analogies. I imagined swallows and nightingales in aerial somersaults and listened to the entablature of emotion, as though the acrobatic birds played upon the strings of unseen, silent lutes. I felt the freshness of the Water in my hair, felt the air kiss it away and knew that somewhere near its source in Densingthal was my answer. I climbed onto the bank and lay naked upon the grass and soft bracken until I grew cold. So I wrapped myself in my blanket and fell peacefully asleep.

In the morning, I did not wish to draw attention to myself by making a fire, although Helga had given me a flint and knife. But as I chose my clothes, I decided not to hide anymore, and so I dressed as you see me. This is not the purple dress from Spandau. I had lost that long ago, but this one reminds me of it. I combed my hair and set out to find the path into the dale.

I was not alone. Not more than thirty steps into searching, I saw a man and his cows rounding a corner. He was an older man with white hair and a long beard. He wore a broad green hat decorated with pheasant feathers. He walked with a long straight ash crook, and whistled as he came.

I thought of what Helga had said, hoping that it was the once-legendary Willi Dörscher, Modran's oft-used excuse, and now walking straight up to me in all his flesh. I quickly laid out the blanket with some wine and sausages.

It *was* Willi. He had cheese with him of course, and was seemingly glad of my company.

"Good morning, sir."

"Good morning, miss. Are you lost? I do not usually meet women such as yourself here."

"I am traveling through here and it is strange, I will grant you that. I am looking for someone, but I think I may have found someone I was not looking for, but perhaps should have a long time ago."

"Hmm. Oh yes. I know you. You are Miss Ada! The scribner woman."

"Are you Willi Dörscher, by any chance?"

"I am."

"Then please join me, will you? I would like to ask your favor."

"I can try, Miss Ada, but I do not know what I could do."

"Please, it is only a few questions."

"In that case, I should be pleased. I am a bit hungry."

He sat down near me and we ate and talked.

"Now this is a pleasant breakfast. You were saying you were looking for someone. A man. Your man? Someone said you had found a man. That was a long time ago, but I remember. That made me glad, for a time. Because those times you wrote out the bills of sale for these cheeses you always looked so sad and lonely. You seemed like a princess from a story my grandmother would tell. She liked to talk of Spain and islands in the Mediterranean where it is warmer, I understand."

"You—you were a customer?" I asked.

"Oh yes, but we cowherds and cheesemakers all probably look alike to you."

And I remembered my error of judgment in that

conversation over chocolate. Willi was right, and it crushed me.

"I am going up there: the Densingthal, to where the path runs into the fir trees. I wish to pay a visit to that dale, for I believe there is someone I know up there."

"I wouldn't go up there. That place is old and haunted. Nobody lives there now except for an old woman. Why is it so important for you to go? You won't find your man there."

We ate slowly. Again, I told him my story. It is one reason, Anton, that I can tell it to you so well. Afterward, Willi was silent for a while.

And then: "After Lord Von Duschter was murdered, the man took his coach, bribed his coachman, and you left together. I suppose you have heard this from Miss Helga. The people down there all said it was true; they knew all along you were a witch and were in league with him. Yet I never believed it. The apple orchard was not blasted by blight; his widow did not go mad or kill herself. She did well out of it."

"Yes, I have heard all of that. Did you all really believe I was a witch?"

"Well, there's good witches and bad, is what I mean to say. The people here were afraid of you but they never thought ill of you. The mines produced good ore and the cows gave sweet milk, which is good for cheese. Children didn't go missing, and they generally grew up strong and good. If you were a bad witch, I suppose bad things would have happened. A few of us thought you were a good witch. My cheeses fetched better prices before you left." He smiled and gave me a wink that would have shamed Modran.

I rather liked the idea of being a witch and thought ill of my prejudice toward the village. Perhaps I could have become a real midwife—instead of a midwife of words—and found a peace there. Perhaps had I not been such an insular bitch of resentment, I could have been happy with one of those knotted blonde men.

It was a fleeting, subjunctive dream. Once our breakfast was done, I said to him:" It was a matter of time. Were it not for Modran, and had I remained here, what would have happened when the mines ran out? What would happen when some pestilence killed some cows, or a father beat his son to death in a drunken wrath and then hid the body? They would still need a witch to burn then, Willi. Such is the way of the world. Nothing good ever lasts."

"You will never know one way or the other now. Both forks of that path are now buried, Miss Ada."

"I just have to keep going then?" I smiled.

Willi put his hands on the top of his walking stick. He was thinking hard but not exactly regarding the truth or untruth of my words. I couldn't know what he was thinking. I couldn't read minds, as they all perhaps thought, and so I moved to start the walk up the overgrown pathway.

"This man of yours—what is his name?"

"I have told you: Modran Modral. He said he traded with you for cheese."

"Modran Modral? No young gentleman with that name ever talked to me about my cheese. What did he look like?"

"He was a tall man with a handsome face, strong chin, and eyes of gray. His hair was brown and silver."

Willi looked at me for a long while, then down at the ground where he was poking his staff. When he looked at me again, his expression had changed away from the friendly old man I had known. There was something distant, fierce, and terribly sad.

271

"And did he come to you in the early twilight? And did he seem the most beautiful thing in the world so that you wished to breathe his breath for the rest of your life? Would you have let him eat you so you could swim and sleep in his belly? Did the very stones sing like birds when he walked near you and you learned all of the old secrets of the world, its making, its undoing, and the dreams of the gods?"

"How do you know?"

"My wife knew him, I think. Or someone like him. It was when she was younger. But his pause was brief with her. A night or two, but she was touched. I was merely the man who loved her and gave her sons and a house, but he took her heart and he keeps it elsewhere. It is a beautiful heart; I remember it. Kill him, if you see him. I think it will get me my wife back. Be careful in the dale. Here, take some more cheese. I remember that you always fancied it, though I do not know where you put it."

I bent down and kissed his cheek. Willi smiled sadly, then turned and walked down the track to Visingotha.

The woody swath in the dale could not have been more than a hundred yards wide, yet in the middle of it, sheltered from the wind and yet privy to its correspondence amidst the tree tops, I felt as though I was in the vastest of all forests.

I camped again that night. Before I slept, I took one more drink from the brook, and let myself wander in the visions of the Water. After it had gone from the clear silver black of the reflected sky to opalescent white to clear again, I saw myself walking across a wide steppe, which was covered with the first thin blanket of late autumn's snow. This is a land I have traveled often by Water, and have done so in my waking life as well. I am grateful that my earlier dream travels there were so accurate.

It was a cold beyond bitterness. It was a profound, theological cold. A cold that called every ounce of my body into being, for each part of me fought against death.

In time I came to a frozen river and I saw Modran through the thick Siberian Ice. He was green, wild-haired, fat—but unmistakable. His teeth were pointed and a darker shade of emerald than his skin. Pounding upon the underside of the ice, swearing words I could not hear or understand, he seemed to scream bubbles and fish eggs. So I raised my skirts, squatted over him, and pissed upon his view, which became understandably more jaundiced.

I rather liked this vision, so I nestled into my blanket and had a comfortably deep and dreamless sleep.

In the morning I ate my cheese and stale bread then clambered up until I reached a level place. There I walked beneath the fir trees and strolled until I came into a wide clearing. The Sun sank, and it lit the end of the clearing as though with orange fire. Between two hills was a decrepit hall. Of what manner of architecture had gone into its spirit and flesh, I could not tell. The profuse and overgrown garden around it—the wild apple trees that climbed and fought with one another—obscured its age and look. It was as if each step changed the hall, and the lengthening shadows hinted at its great age, a history spoken in a forgotten language.

I did not call out. I simply walked through a doorframe that once must have held a door. Even the iron hinges had disappeared; only the stone lintel remained to speak that this was a door, an entry in some distant past. The dank boot room of the window hall lay clogged with dust and old swords and discarded tools. I left my boots there, for I wished to walk silently.

In time heard a noise. At first I thought it was the rustle of a dress, and then it sounded like a broom upon old stones. I realized they were both true, for I met a woman there.

"Are you the mistress of this place?"

"No, I am only waiting. The master is upstairs."

"Your master?"

"No, it is he who is here. I do not see him very much, save before the morning when he returns from his travels."

"Are you the wife of Willi Dörscher?"

"Yes, that is my husband. He was here the other day but has returned to the village down below. If you wish to meet with him I suggest you turn around at once. The darkness here is uncertain."

"How long have you been here?"

"I have not left here in many years. I do not travel or quest. I remain and wait. The master and his kind do not sit by distaffs, writing desks, cradles, or stoves," she said. She held on tightly to her broom.

"I have come to speak with the master."

"I do not think that is wise. He is often cross and usually hungry. I would leave."

"But you do not."

"I tend this place. You do not."

"That is true."

She lit a candle, for the Sun had almost set behind the hills.

"I shall not leave. I wish to speak with the master. Will you announce me?"

"No. You have no need of that. I can tell you are

headstrong and will not leave. The stairs are that way, but know before the end that I have warned you."

She moved off into the darkness and left me in the old entry hall with the candle. I found the stairs and ascended.

Many were broken, as though the stone was old, gray, and senile. Yet as I walked up the stairs, the candle flickered and the ghosts of the place came in scents. Oranges first. Then there was cardamom. Then the smell of a child's soiled diaper. Then the sea, which brought the first tears to my eyes, for I knew the salt smell of the living ocean. Then there was the scent of vast forests lying below the earth, then the smell of coal. I smelled the winds that blew across the mountains when there were no men here. I smelled the red turn of the Sun and then the last smell: the bluest ultramarine of my favorite time. I reached the open door. Beyond was the dim light of the evening: blue as well. I walked into your window hall. And Modran is not here. And now you know the story.

The End of the Riddle

Anton then speaks: "But is that the same thing as the answer? I feel as though you have been asking me the question all along."

"You have an answer, don't you? You asked me the first riddle."

"This man whom you think I know and whom I may know—but I may not—"

"He said this was his house."

"Did he? Did he give you an exact description of where it stands?"

"What other house is there?"

"There are many houses here. The bats and the rats certainly consider this their house. The owls may consider this one of many houses, when they come and stay as the occasional apocalypse for the rats. The old woman downstairs who milks the sheep and goats, this is her house as well. And besides, this man was a liar, Ada."

"Yet he knew there was a grand hall here."

"A fair guess. But I can smell that your line of questioning won't stop, so I will tell you."

"Please do. I have been waiting all night."

"There are many of my kind who have become so like to your kind that you would not know the difference. They have stolen things from you—your language, your love, your avarice, your memories—and have made them their own. Most of all, I believe they have learned to lie."

"Then Modran is of your kind."

"I did not say that, but I must admit that it would be difficult for even me to tell the difference."

"How?"

"Because it doesn't really matter: whether this man was of your flesh or the flesh of the mountains. He is all the same to you. You know this. You have travelled widely and had many men beyond this oh-so-important one. Are they really any different?"

"Yes. Know that I am a rarity in travel, Anton. Even though women in our lands are more free, own property, and sometimes use their own their names, most women do not travel. Though I have not seen Modran since that night in Spandau, I learned an important lesson from him. It buried itself like a toad in the winter, and it slept there in my cold soul for quite a few years. Inside its head is a jewel in the darkness of the cold winter mud, and it is this: my heart was broken, it is true. But I am glad I had a heart to break.

"I have traveled far and learned to trust toad-men: good men who ate flies with thoughts of summer gardens on their minds. Like me, they were not beautiful, but they also hide that jewel in their skulls. They took up residence in the interstitial places between the stones in the walls of my being and so are loyal friends. I still know some of them. A few of the toads I kissed into princes, for a night or a month, and one for quite some time. We would need a long winter's night for you to hear that story.

"Some I shared dreams with. We did not speak our dreams, but we held each other in sleep. But there are few of them, and sometimes I think the Gods gave me five fingers on my purple hand that I may count them all. Only one was as tall as I am. Was there a core of hope for more? I had dreamed it was deep inside of me and that their seed may awaken it into a new child. Yet it never happened, over all of these years, and I can only conclude that I am barren. When I was younger, when purpose was important, I gave purpose to my barrenness."

"Yes, but you cannot smell it yourself, can you? Or I wonder. Did you choose not to smell it?"

"I never would have had Modran's child, nor any other man's. You know this, Anton."

"No, you wouldn't have. Does that give you comfort? Now you can be as selfish and alone as I am. How you squandered your days of misery, the nights of loneliness, never realizing they were your home. You built it timber by timber, wattled it with the old mud of self-regard."

"I wanted that life to end, of that I remember," I say.

He grows larger in his old skinless body. Gone is any shred of humanity now. His fingers become claws; his feet and legs and penis are searching tentacles; his face is now fully equine and fierce.

"And yet was that not a lie to the darkness?" he asks. "You gave your cabin shape, and it shaped you: a friendly home of long legs, long nose, and black hair to flutter on the mountains. And yet you abrade it in this 'narrative' of yours

279

as some sort of prison. Likewise the flatlands where a river was something to cross. The boys who swam in it knew better."

"So, too, the girls who cast their wishes into it as it flowed: wishes like flowers floating on the surface. Of course I wished for joy like those girls I never was." I say.

"A river does not break," Anton says. "It always moves. It speaks in sharp cataracts, and those impress the dull and tired: the distracted people. But what does the greater depth say to ears that are deep enough to hear? That is why the Waterpeople let you pass through their realm untouched—unstained—for you were already stained. Do not pout; it is unbecoming a woman your age, and you know I'm right. You chased after this impossible man because he was like your father. You ran away from Hagen to find him, and you did, in a way."

"I did not run away from Hagen to find my father, because in a way, I was my father, and now I am more than him."

"Then you have your answer. Why are you laughing?"

"Because," I say. "You professed an ignorance of how our minds work and yet you speak clearly and shrewdly: you have great insight into my heart. Anton, you have helped me understand. Memories are not what was. Memories appear faulty and wrong because time creates contradictions, reversals. Yet my desires and thoughts were not illusions at the time, nor are they now, because I am remembering now. It is the truth of the nightingale's stone."

"I do not understand you."

"Narrative, speaking, telling. It is now. It is always now—just as this conversation is—yet it goes over things that happened a long time ago, or just then. So whenever I remember and speak it, it is part of my now; it is why we must tell stories and affix our meaning to them, which is what narrative is."

"If you don't?"

"We would not *be*. We would only exist as records, perhaps."

"Like one thing that follows another, with you as the little spider who forms the most gossamer of connections between them," he says.

"That is because I have to run between the things themselves, and I can barely see them with my dim spider-eyes. To you, it may or may not make sense, but it is a matter of eating or starving: of life or death."

"And yet I can pass through these strings as though they were not even there."

"But you are not a fly, and they are metaphor. Nevertheless, they stick to you. You see there are some filaments on your arms and floppy ears. Some may be on your tongue, for you just made a metaphor yourself. It is what we do with the borrowed strings in the garden that is important."

"What is this garden?"

"You know it. It is Elsewhere, and the outer wall is always the horizon. You claim to live on the other side, beyond time, but now I see you clearly, Anton. Yes, I hear the voices of many others in your whispers. All those who whispered at me, hissed at me—but did they really? You cast doubt, for that is what you are best at. You are the accuser, the slanderer, the rational man, the denier, the practical discourager. I know who you are and who you always were in my life. Why do you retreat? Are you not far vaster and stronger than I am? You have no answers, only doubts. It's why you are wrong about my father and I have won the game. Time has liberated me from past, just as it has liberated me from you. While you were listening, I was watching the stars."

"It does not matter. I am hungrier than ever. You must know that we Laestrygonians do not keep to our word and eat your kind with relish."

"It is a pity then that you had to wait to have me for breakfast, for there is the rising Sun. May it turn you into stone."

The Sun breaks over the mountains and pours into the roofless hall.

"You b—" Anton stops as his throat seizes into granite.

What was he going to say? "You beautiful creature"? "You better be lying"? Perhaps he was going to say, "You bedbug," or, "You bit of saucy ass?" There is the more common metaphor of course, but it is a poor reflection on myself as a teacher if the only term he could pull out of his cyclopean experience was an uncouth, cynical word like that.

I study him for a time and wish for something to remember him by. I never had anything of the sort from Modran. Downstairs, amongst the old tools in the boot room, I find a mason's hammer.

I climb upon his hideous form. The stone of him is smooth and pleasant, though, like a freshly carved statue. It almost pains me. I take the hammer and break off his ear: once flippery and supple as the cool skin of a salamander but now turgid stone. Inside the ear, I can hear his invasions, observations, inventions, tales, whispers, trespasses, and stolen memories.

Smiling, I walk away from him. I shall write all of this down.